The Princess of Convenient Plot Devices

3

Mamecyoro

Illustration by
Mitsuya Fuji

YEN
ON

New York

The Princess of Convenient Plot Devices

Mamecyoro   Illustration by **Mitsuya Fuji**

Translation by **Sarah Moon**

WATASHI WA GOTSUGO SHUGI NA KAIKETSU TANTO NO OJO DEARU Vol.3
©Mamecyoro 2020
First published in Japan in 2020 by KADOKAWA CORPORATION, Tokyo.
English translation rights arranged with KADOKAWA CORPORATION, Tokyo through TUTTLE-MORI AGENCY, INC., Tokyo.

English translation © 2023 by Yen Press, LLC

Yen On
150 West 30th Street, 19th Floor
New York, NY 10001

Visit us at yenpress.com
facebook.com/yenpress
twitter.com/yenpress
yenpress.tumblr.com
instagram.com/yenpress

First Yen On Edition: August 2023
Edited by Yen On Editorial: Leilah Labossiere
Designed by Yen Press Design: Andy Swist

Yen On is an imprint of Yen Press, LLC.
The Yen On name and logo are trademarks of
Yen Press, LLC.

The publisher is not responsible for websites (or
their content) that are not owned by the publisher.

ISBNs: 978-1-9753-5287-5 (paperback)
        978-1-9753-5288-2 (ebook)

10 9 8 7 6 5 4 3 2 1

LSC-C

Printed in the United States of America

Library of Congress Cataloging-in-Publication Data

Names: Mamecyoro, author. | Fuji, Mitsuya, illustrator. |
Moon, Sarah (Translator), translator.
Title: The Princess of Convenient Plot Devices /
Mamecyoro ; illustration by Mitsuya Fuji ; translation
by Sarah Moon.
Other titles: Watashi wa gotsugou shugi na kaiketsu tantou
no oujo dearu. English
Description: First Yen On edition. | New York, NY :
Yen On, 2022– |
Identifiers: LCCN 2022037172 | ISBN 9781975352837
(v. 1 ; trade paperback) | ISBN 9781975352851
(v. 2 ; trade paperback) | ISBN 9781975352875
(v. 3 ; trade paperback)
Subjects: CYAC: Fantasy. | Reincarnation—Fiction. |
Characters in literature—Fiction. | Brothers and
sisters—Fiction. | Gay people—Fiction. |
LCGFT: Fantasy fiction. | Gay fiction. | Light novels.
Classification: LCC PZ7.1.M359 Op 2022 |
DDC [Fic]—dc23
LC record available at https://lccn.loc.gov/2022037172

The Princess of Convenient Plot Devices

Alexis

Esfia's second prince. Octavia's confidant and beloved little brother. Currently away on a mission.

Sirius

The crown prince of Esfia and the soon-to-be king. Has a strained relationship with Octavia.

Sil Burks

The main character of the BL novel *The Noble King* and Sirius's boyfriend. He ventures to the junior ball with Octavia in hopes of learning about his true lineage.

Rust Byrne

The eldest son of Viscount Byrne. Octavia was going to ask him to be her (fake) boyfriend, but…

Leif Nightfellow

The current head of House Nightfellow. Deeply revered by Octavia, who calls him Uncle Dearest.

Derek Nightfellow

Duke Nightfellow's son and Sirius's friend. He also watches over Sil.

Meet the characters of *The Princess of Convenient Plot Devices.*

Octavia

A former high schooler (and *fujoshi*) who was reincarnated into the world of the BL novel *The Noble King*. She's the princess of Esfia, fighting to thwart the arranged marriage in her future!

Klifford Alderton

Octavia's bodyguard. His past is shrouded in mystery. He forged an Adjutant-Sovereign pact with Octavia.

32

Octavia, Esfia's crown princess with memories of her past life—that is who I am now.

With a renewed sense of purpose, I beheld what lay ahead of me. I paused in the entryway of the pleasaunce hall and opened Blackfeather. *Time to pull yourself together, Princess!*

Lieche orchids adorned my hair. *May they bless me with good fortune!*

The golden mask was already back on my face. My makeup was retouched to perfection! The faint red circles beneath my eyes that couldn't be covered were actually a charm point, you see. Even if I removed my mask, surely few would realize I was crying my eyes out just a little while ago! *Mhmm, niiice.*

I was quite satisfied with the skill of the makeup assistants here! I had always assumed that Sasha and my other handmaids of the castle were unbeatable... But now I'm not so sure.

Now I could see why Paradise in the Sky was such a popular venue. Naturally, however, I did owe some of the credit to the savviness of this junior ball's host—Countess Rosa Reddington!

Moving on...

I looked up at Klifford, who was standing beside me. He now donned a white uniform—one that also served as a guard's uniform. These were kept at the venue in order to accommodate requests from the royal family if they were to attend.

"Klifford...do forgive me for being such a handful." I finally apologized to my bodyguard. "I acted so carelessly."

I was the reason he had changed into the white uniform in the first place—I'd stained his bodyguard's uniform with my tears.

"As long as I can move without hindrance, Your Highness, it is not a problem."

"Well, though it might be okay with you..."

One look at Klifford in the uniform, and I couldn't help but let my true feelings leak out. The female party staff had been abnormally fussy about what clothes to give Klifford to change into. And this white uniform was what they had settled on. With gold embellishments and buttons, its design was a bit excessive for a bodyguard. And while a white uniform was the exact opposite of Klifford's usual vibe, a superfine specimen like him pulled it off with style. I could see why the female party staff nodded approvingly at the sight of him.

"Your Highness... Is something amiss?" Klifford asked. He'd caught me staring at him.

"I was merely thinking about how that uniform suits you."

"Is that so?" he asked with a hint of sarcasm.

"Sir Knight... One for you as well." It was the man at the door who was handing out the masks. He handed Klifford a new mask. I suppose there was a pause after he'd said "Sir Knight" because Klifford's uniform had changed.

And his mask would change in turn. Instead of the black mask he'd worn the first time we came to the pleasaunce hall, he was now handed a white mask with gold accents to match his uniform. Klifford took the mask from the servant and put it on.

Now, then...

I can't just stand at the entrance all night. I've gotta go out there... I know I've got to...but...

My anxiety was on a whole new level this time. I wished someone would give my back a little push.

"Klifford... Would you escort me to the center of the pleasaunce hall?" I asked, my eyes straight ahead.

"Your hand, Highness." He extended his hand.

I rested mine on top of his.

The moment we stepped into the pleasaunce hall, hushed whispers and sharp gazes followed us.

"Are those real flowers in her hair?"

"Why, they're Lieche orchids!"

As I heard those snippets of gossip, I was slammed with the reality that nobody in high society wears real flowers in their hair unless they want to stick out like a sore thumb. Then again, with Blackfeather in my hand, that ship had already sailed!

"That young lady... She's the princess, right?"

"I see her bodyguard changed clothes as well."

"She's wearing real flowers in her hair...but strangely enough, it suits her..."

Even in a mask, my identity was painfully obvious. As Klifford guided me, I held Blackfeather to my mouth and sent out my best Princess Smile to the crowd.

I walked on, in search of Rust... I wasn't sure if he was still here. But this was the only place where there was still that possibility. Rust *had* technically accepted my invitation to speak... It's just—I'd awkwardly ran away the moment I saw his face.

If he's not in the pleasaunce hall... Well, I'll cross that bridge when I get to it. Back at the castle, I can always talk to Rust's little brother who serves our army. I might also be able to communicate with him through Houghie like last time.

I looked over all the masked party guests who were dancing. Rust was…not among them. Then I happened to glance at the wall… And like a needle into fabric, my gaze stuck fast.

There he is… Leaning against the wall, glass in hand, Rust had perfectly blended in with the scenery. But there was no way I could ever forget what he looked like.

And he noticed me, too. He raised his glass, intending to nod to me…but then he froze. Did he freeze…because he saw me? His mask was hiding his expression, so I couldn't tell for sure. But he raised his glass again at me—this time for real. And my hand, loosely resting on top of Klifford's, switched to a firm squeeze.

Snap out of it, Octavia! Don't falter!

"Thank you, Klifford. You may leave me here," I told him once I'd walked a little closer to Rust. I released his hand, and I felt a twinge of helplessness… *No, it's all in my head.*

"Forgive me for the intrusion…"

Rust was conversing with two gentlemen I didn't know. Even without their masks, I wouldn't have recognized them anyway. But they were Khangenans…I think? They had three circular earrings in their left ears—that's supposed to be traditional Khangenan style.

In the past, when tensions between Esfia and its neighbor were at their height, Khangenans who wore their traditional earrings to an Esfian royal ball were berated for disrespecting the crown. I'd been taught that this was the spark that caused the war. Either the Khangenans were intentionally provoking Esfia, or Esfians had used the earrings as an excuse to attack—the story varied greatly, depending on which side you asked.

Ideally, I'd speak with Rust alone, but I didn't want to make a bad impression on the Khangenans…

I held my fan in both hands and smiled sweetly. "Khangenans, welcome to my kingdom. Would you mind if I joined in on your conversation?"

"Your Highne—! It's quite all right."

"I hope *we* are not an intrusion, Your Highness."

They both curtly excused themselves.

"Oh dear… Did I interrupt an entertaining conversation?"

"No, you interrupted a *boring* conversation… So no worries, Princess." Rust, now alone, peeled himself off the wall.

When I saw him freeze at the sight of me earlier…was that just my imagination? He's acting totally normal right now.

His voice… It didn't sound like that mysterious man's voice. I think. So it's not him. I'd decided to face him…but *that silhouette…*

At least his face is hidden by that mask. Maybe I'll be able to remain calm around him. The only problem remaining is…what's his relationship to that mysterious man?

"You said earlier that you wished to be alone… Are you all right now?"

"Yes, the matter has been dealt with."

"Well, I'm pleased to hear it."

"I apologize for my abrupt departure in the middle of our dance. I suppose you were startled by it?"

"Yes, Your Highness. I worried that I had perhaps done something to offend you."

"And did you wait for me to return?"

"Was it not *you*, Princess, who asked to speak with me through my brother?"

"Well…was it not *you* who had something to tell *me*?"

Rust shut his mouth. And deep behind the opaque glass in his mask, I swear I could see his amber eyes staring hard at me.

We both had things we wished to say. It's just, there were far too many people around us to have an in-depth conversation.

I looked at Rust, cool as a cucumber. "Might I suggest…we change locations?"

I wasn't the only one who wished to avoid speaking further around curious ears, so Rust had accepted my invitation to relocate. While I'd entered the pleasaunce hall in a pair, I left in a trio. Rust was the only one of us still wearing a mask—his insistence, for some reason. And as I wanted to put off looking at his bare face as long as possible, I didn't complain.

Incidentally, nobody we passed on our way out did a double take at the sight of my bare face. Then again, they were distracted by the well-placed arrangement of Lieche orchids in my hair—between that and the makeup wizardry, the fact that I'd been crying was perfectly camouflaged.

Relief washed over me...for only an instant. Another part of me was still drowning in worry. I was the one who had suggested to Rust that we relocate. That meant it was my job to take us somewhere I had in mind to talk... But where the hell was that? As we walked down the corridor, I racked my brain trying to think of discreet places we could go to discuss things...

That's right! I confess! I was so preoccupied psyching myself up for Confrontation with Rust, the Sequel being that I had no plans on *where* exactly we were going to have said Confrontation!

The VIP lounge was always an option... But if it was already in use, that would mean we'd have to kick out whoever was in there. Then perhaps we could make use of one of the private rooms I'd used as a temporary crying refuge earlier?

Yeah, no... I'm not too wild about the idea of going back there... Bringing Rust with me to a place I'd retreated to for solitude holds some implications I'm not too comfortable with, y'know?

And merely the act of leaving the pleasaunce hall with Rust (and Klifford) by my side made all the other guests stare real hard at us already.

So I avoided the private rooms and settled on the corridor facing the garden. Between all the crying and makeup fixing, a lot of time had lapsed since the junior ball had begun—the sun was already about to set.

Paradise in the Sky's famous garden was dyed orange by the setting sun and illuminated softly by the square lanterns. It was quite beautiful…yet easy for a directionally challenged person like myself to get lost in.

Huh… How about the garden?

Alec and I took a walk there once. There was a cute little gazebo, too. It was a lovely little nook to have a relaxing moment with someone. Yup. I'd found my spot!

Which way was the gazebo? Hmmm… Let's see, go straight along the path where the garden guards are standing, and—

I stopped in the corridor and scanned the garden left to right.

Wait a minute… Where are the guards?

"What's the matter, Princess? Is something bothering you?" Rust asked.

I shook my head. "No, I'm fine. There's a gazebo in the garden—let's have our chat there."

"Of all places…you're taking us to the *garden*?"

Rust's reaction sounded weird…I think. *What did he mean by "of all places"? Well, I can't really think of anywhere better than the garden anyway… No, yeah. I'm gonna commit to it!*

"Why, yes. Come along."

Since my landmark guards were missing, I was worried I would get lost…but I managed to take us to the gazebo Alec and I had discovered! I was heaving some pretty epic sighs of relief in my brain, let me tell you.

As we stepped through the flowery arch, we came upon the hexagon-roofed wooden gazebo, which was illuminated by the square lanterns. And just as I'd planned, there wasn't a soul in sight.

Rust and I sat across from each other on some chairs in the gazebo. Klifford stood on my left-hand side. And then…I started the conversation.

"Might I ask you to remove your mask?"

"If you command it of me, Your Highness…," Rust answered calmly, removing his mask and quietly setting it down on the table.

Last time I saw his face, it was so sudden that my mind went blank.

But this time, I was prepared for it. I still trembled a little, but the shock wasn't so bad that it sapped my ability to think.

I gave his bare face a good long stare...taking everything in. Aside from his scar, he looked just like that mysterious man. His hair was golden. His eyes were amber. But...on closer inspection... he exuded a completely different vibe. That mysterious man had this sort of...intentionally fake humanness to him. Rust didn't have that.

"You are the second person to be disturbed by the sight of my face, Princess Octavia. So I must ask... Whom do I resemble to you?"

So...Rust doesn't know who he resembles?

Also, he said I was the *second* person who was disturbed by the sight of him... In my case, it was because he looked just like that mysterious man. But nobody else in this world should know about that mysterious man besides me...right? Nobody else would know...

No, wait a minute, maybe he's baiting me?

I opened my fan, firmly gripping its center.

We're probably both feeling each other out right now. And since I ran away from him at the start, I'm currently at a disadvantage.

"If you want answers...then shouldn't you ask the first person your face disturbed?"

Rust gave my quippy response an impudent smile. Then he answered slowly, "You mean to say I should ask...His Majesty the King?"

Wait...the "first person" in question was my father?!

33

I moved my fan slightly, letting its fluffy feathers help me keep my composure.

My father... Did he meet the mysterious man, too? In other words...

I looked at Rust, the man I was confronting. If I took his words at face value, that meant there was at least one other person besides him…who existed IRL?

A person who looks just like him…

"Yes. That is exactly what I mean." Rust drew his chin inward.

"What do you mean by…that's exactly what you mean?"

"Princess Octavia. I suppose you can guess what feature most people notice the first time they see my face?" Rust asked, touching the distinctive scar along the left side of his brow. When he touched it, the scar disappeared behind his hand. This scar was the one distinguishing feature I had to go off of to determine whether this was the real Rust Byrne of my beloved BL series, *The Noble King*.

"Most people notice this scar before they see the shape or features of my face. I was born with this scar—and I've noticed a great variety of reactions from those who see it. Some consider it a gift from God… Others see it as an omen. But everyone has one thing in common— they show their reactions to my scar in their eyes immediately upon seeing it. Naturally, some people pretend they don't notice my scar. But the only exceptions…"

Rust removed his hand from his scar, revealing it again. "Neither you nor His Majesty paid any mind to my scar. Now, perhaps you were both graciously ignoring it as royalty should… Except neither of you had *no* reaction to it, either. You were both greatly affected by me—no, by my overall appearance—*not* by my scar."

"Perhaps it is because your face is quite handsome?"

"I am deeply humbled, Your Highness. However, what you just said makes the whole situation all the more peculiar. When you and His Majesty saw my face…you recoiled. Almost as if you had seen an apparition of someone who should not exist. You looked at me not with fondness—far from it."

An apparition of someone who should not exist…

If he was only describing me, I'd totally get it. I think I let my emotions show pretty clearly.

But…my father?

Even in his personal life, my father was never easy to read. Part of that was because he was the king. So I couldn't possibly imagine my father—a king—meeting the son of a viscount and showing emotion...and so strongly, besides.

"The king and the princess are at the center of the kingdom. And both were abnormally disturbed by the sight of my face... Isn't it only natural to find that fascinating?"

The way he talks... Is Rust completely unrelated to that mysterious man? Am I actually supposed to believe that he just happened to be born with that copycat face by coincidence?

"I wonder... Is that really all there is to it?" I asked. *Don't you "find it fascinating" because of some reason that goes much deeper than that? I still haven't gotten over my suspicions of you yet.*

Rust answered immediately. "Yes. That's all there is to it." He sounded quite natural.

"Well, what about you? Whom do *you* think you resemble? I'm curious to know."

"If I name a significant person...then would you perhaps bring about a change to the situation I'm in?"

He probably meant to make a bargain with me. But what he said was already a huge bounty to me—I knew he had some idea of whom he resembled.

So...there's another one of him.

I definitely wanted to ask him just who this "significant person" was. Were they Esfian? Or from another country, perhaps? And what's more, since he did say "person," that meant it had to be someone who actually existed—not some fictitious character.

Regardless, I could think of no other *significant person* to me other than that mysterious man.

I was about to accept his bargain—but a little voice in my head shut me up at the last minute. *What, exactly, is the "situation" Rust is in? And does he really think I can get him out of it? The details to both questions are still unknown, Octavia—you shouldn't make a flimsy promise!*

"I cannot guarantee that I can change whatever situation you are in."

"I am well aware of that. If I may be frank, Your Highness, if you had agreed to my proposal outright, I would have walked away then and there."

Yikes... I sure dodged a bullet! I was, like, super close to totally saying yes, good sir!

"I cannot trust anyone who blindly accepts a bargain when they aren't certain they can follow through with their end of it. It proves they are a dunce at negotiations."

Dang, Rust... Even if you're not that mysterious man, I still get the sense you're a formidable foe.

"Rust Byrne. Tell me... Why did you wish to speak with me?"

"Unlike Houghie...the Viscount Winfell, House Byrne has nothing to gain by forging a relationship with you, Your Highness. However, when the princess of Esfia herself expresses a desire to make contact with me—the son of a lowly viscount—wouldn't it be stranger of me to *ignore* the invitation? Especially when she had a reaction to my scar much like the king himself."

Rust paused there. "Now. I ask *you*, Your Highness... What do *you* want of *me*?"

His question almost made me look away, so I awkwardly covered my face with my fan. After all, the reason I wanted to meet with Rust was so I could say *"Be my fake boyfriend!"* But at present...I wasn't really feeling the desire to ask him to play that role.

Even if I charmed him into saying yes, the idea of having a boyfriend (albeit, a fake one) who looked exactly like that mysterious man... Well, it made my stomach churn. I'd probably have a hard time trusting anything he said, for that matter.

Wait...huh? Let's think about that from a different angle... Wouldn't it actually be *more* advantageous to keep him close to me as my fake boyfriend *because* he's like that? *Hmmm... Should I go with the original plan and ask Rust to be my fake boyfriend? Or should I just drop it and look for someone else?*

"By the way, Your Highness... You certainly have domesticated quite the dangerous specimen."

Rust's sudden observation broke through my frazzled thoughts. I followed his gaze. There was only one thing in his line of vision: Klifford.

A "dangerous specimen"? And from the way he said "domesticated," it's hard to take that as anything but an insult.

Klifford was keeping watch over the eastern side of the garden, rather than on us. But he immediately looked our way and nodded.

The east... Where the absent guards are supposed to be?

Rust looked in my direction...but our gazes didn't meet. "Many high-ranking nobles—sometimes royalty—use Paradise in the Sky to receive guests. Don't you think the security in this garden is a bit light? A momentary negligence, perhaps?"

Well, if I noticed security was abnormally light, of course Rust felt suspicious about it.

"Surely there was a reason for it... Guards aren't negligent—it's their job not to be. We are perfectly safe, I assure you." I made my tone as confident as possible, trying to give this garden my seal of approval.

"Furthermore, you keep your bodyguard by your side, Your Highness?"

"Well, Klifford is *always* by my side." Like Rust said, he's my personal bodyguard. And Klifford is passionately devoted to his job... much like the staff at this venue, I guess. I mean, yeah, I do think it's kinda strange that the garden guards aren't here, but as someone who personally received the staff's thorough makeover treatment, I can vouch that they are *not* negligent!

Surely, the guards at Paradise in the Sky also have a strong work ethic. They'd never leave their posts or ditch their jobs for no reason! Like, there must be some *positive*, venue-related reason why there aren't many garden guards right now! Though...I can't exactly think of what that reason could be.

"Indeed, they are not negligent... It seems everything is going according to plan, and the mouse is caught in their trap."

Uh...huh?

My brain was a hodgepodge of question marks. I think Rust and I are crossing wires here!

"Ah yes. It has begun." Rust turned toward the eastern side of the garden.

And in direct contrast with Rust's calm, cool tone of voice...from the very direction Klifford had been wary of all this time, I started to pick up the sounds of an angry roar. Along with...the clashing of swords. Klifford shifted his stance and placed his hand on his sword hilt. He was prepared for the worst.

Our view of the garden from the gazebo didn't change a bit. The flowers, blooming in white, red, yellow, blue...continued to shine beautifully in the lantern lights. But something disturbing was happening in the eastern side of the garden... I could hear it in the air.

"It has begun"? What has begun?

"When you first set foot in the garden, Your Highness, I wondered how things would unfold... But it turns out this gazebo is in an extraordinary position. Do you not find our view to be epically lacking?"

Rust seemed to know exactly what was happening in the east end of the garden... But I was still completely clueless. All I knew was that I heard something quite different from the swordplay in the castle training grounds. The heavy...raw sounds of real fighting resounded in the distance.

I psyched myself up inside to be strong—ironically, it was because of Rust. I couldn't stand the thought of someone who looked just like the mysterious man seeing me cower in fear. It was a matter of pride. Besides, if I wanted to know what was going on, as Rust seemed to have a grasp of the situation, it was best that I just ask him.

"Um, may I ask what is happening?"

"The anti-royalist intruders have revealed themselves. Khangena is backing them. So Countess Reddington provided us with this space so that we—with Duke Nightfellow at the lead—could crack down on them. Except we had one problem: When were the restless traitors going to come out of hiding and make their move? The key to everything...was you, Your Highness.

"The crown princess of Esfia is an attractive target for the traitors. If you were to attend the junior ball, we knew they would make their move. That's why we lightened security in one area of the venue. So we could lure the pests out of their nest with the enticing aroma of your sweet nectar, Octavia, and make a wholesale arrest of the traitors and all the guests that are connected with them. Your Highness—did you not become the decoy of your own volition?" Rust smiled mirthfully. "You event went so far as to bring Sil Burks with you."

"I... All I did was accept Countess Reddington's invitation." *You're way...way off, my dude!*

"Yes, I suppose you did. And when you agreed to perform the opening dance, the countess got a far bigger catch than she ever dreamed of. Ordinarily, mistakenly letting traitors into her junior ball would have been quite the scandal, but as luck would have it, the net she spread managed to catch the traitors. Once the full story comes to light, I'm sure she'll receive quite a lot of praise for it."

Did my dad know about this? Yeah...I'm sure he did. It sounds like a pretty elaborate plan, so it's highly likely he knew about it. But then he could've at least clued me in about it when I said yes to the countess's invitation!

Unless it was that thing where you have to sometimes keep your allies in the dark in order to trick your enemy? Yeah, I'll admit if I had known about the plan, I'm not sure I would've been able to give a convincing performance...

But wait a minute. Why was Rust so familiar with the plan? Forget about the mysterious man for a second—let's just see what we remember about Rust Byrne, the character. He's the eldest son of Viscount Byrne...a house of anti-royalists. A character in direct opposition to Sil and Sirius.

"Those *restless traitors* you mentioned... Rust Byrne, just which side are you on?"

"An outrageous question, indeed." Rust pressed his hand to his heart. "I investigated those traitors and aided the crackdown—that's the side I'm on. Now, I *could* have divulged Countess Reddington's plan to the traitors if I had wanted to...but I worked on the countess's side."

"Then, pray tell, who were the Khangenans you were conversing with in the pleasaunce hall?"

In light of everything you've told me, those friends of yours seem just a tad sus.

"They were potential traitors, you might say. They learned of the traitors' scheme and wanted to assist them. Your sudden attendance served as a litmus test for that. Guests who had initially turned down the invitation but came here at the last minute became prime suspects. That is why this junior ball was held right around the same time as the Council of Feudal Lords—a time when nobility from all over the land gather at the royal capital."

Which means nobody was caught flat-footed from a sudden invasion, right? The clamor I was hearing in the east was the result of Uncle Dearest and Countess Rosa's plan going *well.*

"However, traitors are skilled at thinking up nefarious plans. We may have caught the anti-royalists in our net as planned. But as for the other traitors...the ones with a different target...what do you suppose happened to them?"

Is he saying what I think he's saying—?

"Stop them! Capture them all alive!" A voice much louder than the rest shot through the air from the direction of the clamor.

No sooner did the voice shout out than a group of men emerged from the bushes. There were three in total, swords drawn. And when they saw me in the gazebo, they charged without hesitation.

I'm such a dumbass! I shouldn't have chosen the garden! If only I'd known about their plan in advance... Welp, too late now!

But wait! I actually......have no fighting ability whatsoever. And Rust—who surely could hold his own in a fight against Sirius—was still sitting all chill at the table. His legs were crossed, and his eyes were eager—like he was there as a spectator. Well, some good *he'll* be in a fight...

Which means it's Klifford against three men?

G-god, what do we do? I don't care how strong Klifford is. Won't he get hurt? Is there some way I can even the playing field for him? Or would I just risk making things worse?

"Your Highness, should I take them alive?" Klifford asked, cool as ever (while I was freaking out right next to him).

O-okay! I shouldn't let myself lose it at a time like this. I have to answer Klifford's question...take them alive? "Capture them all alive!"— isn't that what the side against the traitors was saying?

Stay calm. Be cool, Octavia. "Why, yes. As long as doing so will not encumber you."

"As you wish, Your Highness. This will take but a moment." And with that, Klifford yanked his sword—sheath and all—out of his belt. The three men were closing in on him.

Was it because I told him to keep them alive? Klifford's sword was still in its sheath, and the approaching traitors were laughing at him for it.

"Klifford! Draw your sword—" But I was cut off right there.

He was clearly outnumbered. There were three men with naked swords against Klifford, who had a sheathed sword. And yet in spite of those circumstances...it unfolded like a badass fight scene in an action movie.

One by one, Klifford picked off the trio of traitors—easily and precisely—completely incapacitating them. Klifford's sword danced like an extension of his body. And there was a splash of martial arts thrown in, too. Every movement was deliberate—it was inhuman.

Until Klifford revealed himself to be one, I had only heard about the legendary Adjutants from stories. Seeing him fight made me realize that this was the very reason why they were dubbed a warrior clan.

In the blink of an eye, the trio of traitors were on the ground, their faces twisted with pain. They were still breathing. They were not bleeding. But they were gasping and moaning, clutching their limbs… They seemed unable to move. And during that short battle, they'd lost all their weapons.

The crisis had passed…for now. I ran over to Klifford.

"Your Highness, I still haven't—"

"Are you hurt?"

I saw the way he fought. His movements were too fast for me to follow, but it was clearly an intense battle. Still, I really wish he hadn't fought armed men with a sheathed sword! It was far too dangerous!

"No."

Since his uniform was white, I could easily tell if he was bleeding. And yeah, he looked okay.

"I know I asked you to leave them alive, but that was no reason to keep your sword sheathed."

"Forgive me, Princess… I was worried I would not be able to hold myself back enough."

"I can understand why you would be concerned for your bodyguard's safety, but don't you think he made the right call?" Rust butted in from his seat at the table. "If he had drawn his sword, it's doubtful those traitors would have survived the fight. There was no telling how big the difference between each person's swordplay was. If the gap had been too great, Klifford may have dealt deadly blows to each of them, even if he meant to go easy on them."

"Thank you for praising my bodyguard… Is that what you wish me to say?"

"Yes, Your Highness. Your domestication methods aside, I should not be surprised that you—"

The rest of the words disappeared into his throat, like an interior monologue. But I did catch one thing: ...missary.

Missary? Is that a proper noun? Or part of a proper noun? If that was a complete word on its own, and I simply misheard it, then he was either saying emissary or...misery? Neither really rings a bell...

"Princess Octavia?!" somebody cried out... It was one of the guards who had chased after the three traitors.

34

"That trio is the last of them, Your Highness. All the intruders from the outside have been captured," a stern-looking *ikemen* informed me with a bow as I sat at the table in the gazebo... Even his bow really showed his personality. He had a very stiff, no-nonsense vibe about him.

For some reason...for *some reason*, I was receiving a status report from the field superintendent of the garden in this little traitor-capturing scheme. This guy seems to think that me being at the junior ball was part of the plan all along!

But thanks to his little misconception, I now knew the gist of everything. Some armed outsiders had infiltrated the party and blended in with the invited guests. The traitors we were hoping to capture were split into two groups.

For the group of traitors who sneaked into the junior ball disguised as invited guests, we made them think security was light and prepared an ideal infiltration route for them: Paradise in the Sky's prized garden. That's where the outside group—the armed one—would sneak in. Then they would rendezvous with their friends on the inside. This was the enemy's plan.

But they never got to rendezvous with their friends—we cut them off right at the garden. The only traitors who remained were the ones inside the party, disguised as guests. After a while, they would start to suspect something was amiss, and they would have to show their true colors...

That was our plan, apparently.

The field superintendent—a graying man in his thirties in a white guard's uniform with an aura that just screamed *soldier!*—was waiting for me to answer him.

Wait...huh? I know this guy...

"Excuse me, but are you Duke Nightfellow's...?" I asked him, my mouth half obscured by my fan.

The man's cheeks softened slightly into a smile. "Yes. I serve His Excellency."

"Yes, I thought so." Ha! I was right! So when I saw a familiar face among the sea of guards in the garden, I wasn't tripping! While he *was* dressed in the venue uniform, it did make sense that Duke Nightfellow's personal guard would be among the guards here.

And boy, what a blast from the past, hearing the term *His Excellency...* Uncle Dearest's subordinates call him His Excellency—what a way to show how devoted they are!

Then I heard a clinking noise and looked toward its source.

"Is that...Khangena-made?"

"Look closer. There's a special feature on the blade... This could only be Turchen-made."

"Turchen? Just one of them? Is it real?"

The trio Klifford has just knocked out were tied up by the venue guards as they arrived on the scene. I had already explained to this man why those men were moaning and groaning with their faces in the dirt. Before they were to be transported away, the items in their possession were searched.

"You lot, stop whispering!" the field superintendent barked at the guards who were going over the traitor loot. "Have you forgotten you are in the presence of Her Highness?!"

"Aye, sir! My apologies!"

"My apologies, sir!"

The two guards jumped to attention, shut their mouths, and got back to work.

A Turchen-made weapon...all the way out here...

I had a little think to myself as I watched one concealed weapon after another come to light. It was obvious that the enemy had planned rather thoroughly for this night. And they had Turchen-made weapons, besides?

Turchen was formerly a producer of high-quality weapons. Perhaps it had something to do with the fact that the Adjutants—a sort of endangered species—once lived in great numbers there. But the technology was no longer in use. And while some of Turchen's weapons were still in circulation, a *Turchen-made* weapon evoked an image of something primarily crafted in the past. The weapons varied greatly depending on who made them—a weapon forged by an expert was a highly coveted commodity that sold for huge sums of money.

The trio had seemed weak since Klifford disposed of them so quickly... But what if they were actually pretty strong dudes?

And while we're on the subject, let's talk about the Turchen Arc. As poor Lord Sil gets caught up in a string of dubious deeds, the name Turchen keeps coming up...until at long last, the story's location shifts over to Turchen—that's how the tale goes.

"Your Highness, please forgive us for putting you in grave danger due to our ineptitude." The field superintendent barged into my thoughts with an apology and a deep bow.

I flinched. *Er, if your plan was to lure the intruders in here through the garden by lightening up security, I kinda doubt you'd assume the princess would be in that very garden!*

"Please, don't apologize. You were *not* inept—I fell into the intruders' path due to the choices I made on my own. I only hope I wasn't too much of a hindrance to your plan."

I'm actually genuinely worried about that!

"A hindrance? Oh, Your Highness... Both His Excellency and Countess Reddington instructed us to not step on Your Highness's toes at all this evening."

D-did they, now. It seems that I, and I alone...was left out of the loop! But it would be totally awkward if I said so...

In my mind, I was sweating bullets.

The field superintendent lowered his tone. "Even so, we were also ordered to make an exception if we ever suspected you were likely to be in danger... Did you not receive the same order, Sir?"

His gaze and tone suddenly turned sharp. He was addressing the man who—from the moment the intruders arrived to the moment they were defeated—had stayed on the sidelines and watched: Rust Byrne. It seemed as though the two had had a little talk prior. So I guess that meant when Rust said he was on Countess Reddington's side, he was telling the truth. Except this man was on Uncle Dearest's side, while Rust was on Countess Rosa's side, specifically.

"Her Highness requested that I accompany her to the garden—this is probably a mere difference of opinion. I determined that Her Highness was not in any immediate danger." Rust crossed his legs, leaned back in his chair, and drawled unapologetically.

"But I heard that while you were tasked with protecting the princess, only her bodyguard fought to protect her. You did not get up to fight when the intruders charged at her—how do you explain that?" the field superintendent asked Rust, after acknowledging Klifford, who had withdrawn behind me.

"I was unarmed so that I—as a collaborator—could blend in seamlessly with the other guests. So rather than place my vulnerable self in a fight, wouldn't you say leaving the fighting to the armed man who fights for a living was the more advantageous choice?"

"Yes, why *were* you unarmed?" I asked. "I am most curious to hear your answer." I wouldn't be surprised if Rust had a concealed weapon just in case he needed to fight—he wasn't that careless. And he was technically...my ally?...or so it seemed—though I still resisted the notion on a psychological level—and I'm sure Countess Rosa would have permitted that he carry.

His amber eyes—the eyes that resembled the mysterious man's so uncannily—glanced at me briefly. But he abruptly looked away.

"On the surface, Your Highness, I am attending this junior ball as an invitee. And while I *am* on your side, only a few people know the full details of this. If someone was to discover a weapon on me when nothing was happening, it would cause quite a panic. And some people out there can determine by sight alone when a person is concealing a weapon, as you are well aware."

Determine by sight alone… He's talking about how Derek spotted Klifford's concealed weapon, isn't he?! That reminds me, did Uncle Dearest tell Derek about the plan?

"Naturally, when the traitors reared their ugly heads, I wished I had a weapon on me."

"Funny… You looked rather calm, considering."

"Well, your bodyguard was with us, Your Highness. I *did* feel calm. However, now that the traitors are here, and the fear of my concealed weapon causing a scandal has passed, I do feel nervous remaining unarmed. Will you please loan me a weapon, servant of Duke Nightfellow?"

The superintendent shook his head at Rust's brazen request. "I cannot allow it. Countess Reddington assigned you the role of an unarmed party guest for a reason. We cannot throw a wrench in her plans."

"Ah…very well. Then I suppose I shall have to carry out my role as intended." Rust backed off, seemingly unfazed.

One of the guards who had been waiting nearby stepped in and whispered something in the superintendent's ear. Then the three traitors were dragged away—I guess that meant the inspection was over.

The superintended nodded at his subordinate, then he turned to me. "Your Highness, I'm returning to the main hall—to His Excellency's side. What do you wish to do?"

Huh? Uncle Dearest? Even though I couldn't see myself, I just knew my eyes were sparkling. "I wish..." *To see Uncle Dearest, of course!*

But then something flashed across my mind—the plan to flush out the traitors. *Where exactly am I supposed to be right now? Am I supposed to go to the main hall as a decoy, draw the still-hidden traitors out of hiding, and help Uncle Dearest and his men? Or I should I just learn my lesson from the fiasco in the garden and quietly go wait someplace safe?*

Whenever you're stuck, it's always best to ask somebody who actually knows the plan!

"I wish to act in a way that makes Duke Nightfellow's plan with Countess Reddington run as smoothly as possible. And as someone under the duke's direct command, I wish that you would tell me what I should do."

All I wish is to give a helping hand to Uncle Dearest's team! A helping hand, I say!

"Well—though you were in danger earlier, the garden is now secured. If you would stay here on standby until the threat has been fully quashed, that would be best."

Standby... Yeah, figures...

But I don't know when to quit, so I asked anyway. "Um, would it perhaps be more effective for the plan that I return to the main hall and carry out my role as a decoy there?"

"That would be risky, Your Highness. The traitors among the invited party guests will feel desperate and might try to harm you. The plan's efficacy matters less to me than your safety, Your Highness."

Yeah, I guess if nothing was happening, that would be one thing. But if I slip up now, that would put me in great danger... Seeing Uncle Dearest wasn't my only wish—there was also something I wanted to check on with my own eyes—but oh well.

"I suppose I should take your advice, so I shall. But in exchange..." I decided to bargain a little.

*   *   *

The sun set, and the moon and stars twinkled in the dark sky. The positions of the stars were different from my past-life memories. And even though the moon here shared the same name, it was not the moon I knew. The moon in this world never waned or waxed—it was always full.

I could still see everything clearly in the garden, even at night, due to the light of the square lanterns. There were no traces of the little scuffle Klifford'd had with the traitors. The flowers swayed gently in the night breeze, carrying their sweet fragrance all the way to the gazebo.

It was the epitome of peace. It was so peaceful, in fact, that the row of guards the superintendent had left behind in the distance were a bit of an eyesore. Other than that, the mood in the garden felt just the same as it did before the traitors attacked.

Klifford had stationed himself a little behind me to my left, and Rust sat in front of me at the other end of the table.

Since I had decided to stay in the garden, I'd asked the superintendent if he could carry out a little task for me. It was just a precaution... something I wanted him to do for me so I could rest at ease. And a guard with a somber expression on his face returned immediately and whispered in my ear.

"Thank you... Inform Lord Derek of this at once."

"Yes, Princess!"

After the guard was out of sight, I turned back to Rust—who had been watching us with great interest—and asked bluntly, "Rust Byrne...are you a collaborator in this?"

"If by collaborator, you mean in the plan to capture the traitors, then yes. I did my utmost to serve you, Princess, did I not?"

I closed my fan. "Oh, don't play dumb with me. Before those traitors arrived, you mentioned they had a different target, did you not?"

"Yes, I did."

"Lord Sil's whereabouts are currently unknown."

"Is that what you asked the guard to investigate?"

"Yes, I asked him to check the party hall to see where Lord Sil was." But the guard could not find Sil.

The person who was the most out of place at this junior ball was Sil. My attendance alone wouldn't be enough to get the anti-royalists to make their move.

The anti-royalists had a different target. So…what if that target was Sil? When it was discovered that Sil was missing, that nagging worry of mine became concrete. As did the fact that those traitors were probably already in the party hall.

I knew Derek was keeping a close eye on Sil. If he had just disappeared like that…something nefarious had to be at play. It was the only logical conclusion I could make.

"You purposely guided me to reach this conclusion, did you not? So…I'll ask again. Are you a collaborator?"

Hey, if your language is *that* suggestive, even someone dumb like me will have an epiphany!

"Is that not a needless fear, Your Highness? Isn't it possible that Lord Sil—emboldened by the lack of supervision from Sirius—took the opportunity to sneak off into a room with someone? That sort of thing has happened before, you know."

He was right. In the past, there was a big kidnapping scare at a junior ball…and it turned out the missing man had actually sneaked off into a private room to have a little fun.

However.

"Are you suggesting that Lord Sil would share a flirtatious moment with a man other than my brother?" I snorted. *Not. In. A. Million. Years!*

"And even if someone tried to seduce Lord Sil, he's not the sort of man who would fall for it," I snapped, haughtily pointing my closed fan at Rust's face.

"……" Rust was silent, and his amber eyes widened in disbelief… perhaps from the confidence in my voice.

Well, Sil was like that in the books! And as for the real Sil… Well, today was actually the first time I managed to talk to him without my brother nearby... But I saw my brother and him being a happy couple a lot with my own eyes, okay?!

"Princess... I have a sincere question."

"And what is this *sincere question* of yours?"

"Your Highness... Hasn't it ever crossed your mind to dispose of Sil Burks? If Burks were to disappear into the night, wouldn't your little problem be solved?"

Rust was speaking about Esfia's royal family's ways...but from my perspective. The kings marry other men. And their sisters give birth to the heirs...

"Even if I forced Lord Sil out of the picture, the underlying conditions would not change. That would not be enough to resolve my *little problem*."

It would only be a temporary measure, and it would be a rotten way of doing things—leaving nothing but resentment in my wake. My escape—and my escape alone—would be meaningless. Even if Sirius did marry a woman and I was relieved of my task...what if everything went back to square one with the next generation?

"Even if it means a direct confrontation, I intend to follow all the necessary procedures and fight straightforwardly against Lord Sil—no, against my brother Sirius. Now...did that clear up your suspicion?"

"Yes, Your Highness. Now I understand your line of thinking."

"Good."

Then Rust said, out of the blue, "Though I'm not sure you'll trust me...you have my word: I am not a collaborator."

Yup! I don't trust you!

Rust had more to say. "However, it was merely by chance that I got wind of the traitors who are after Sil Burks."

"And did you tell Countess Reddington about this?"

"Why must I tell her? I am indeed aiding her, but only in her plan to capture the anti-royalists. This is a matter that has nothing to do with me."

"Are you trying to tell me...that you are under no obligation to rescue Lord Sil?"

"Wouldn't *that* be exactly the sort of task for Sirius? Or for his friend, the son of Duke Nightfellow?"

"Do you have an inkling of where Lord Sil is right now?"

"I do," Rust answered, all pompous airs dropped.

"Then tell me. Surely that is what you want." *You were the one who gave me the hint, after all.*

"*Is* it what I want? I was just curious—over whether you would abandon Burks. Over whether you brought him to the junior ball...specifically so you could do away with him."

What?!

I froze in shock.

Holy shit, that's terrifying! So wait, Rust thinks I sweetly lured Sil into my carriage knowing full well that there was a plot to capture him? Just what kind of *evil* princess do you take me for?! Your accusations are *false*, good sir! *False!*

Rust, I know you were an evil puppet master sort of character in the books... But isn't your train of thought taking quite a dark turn there?

"Truth be told, I didn't think this would happen. You are not as I imagined you would be, Princess Octavia."

"I've had enough of your impertinence. Are you going to tell me where Lord Sil is?"

For a few seconds, neither of us said anything. His eyes pierced mine, probing my soul. I squinted in suspicion—and not because he was staring at me.

How strange... Ever since he set foot in this gazebo, he hasn't once—

"The one who is after Sil Burks...is most likely an *Adjutant*."

Instead of telling me *where* Sil was, Rust told me *who* was after him.

"We're up against an *Adjutant*, Your Highness... Do you still wish to know where Burks is?"

35

"Why...why is an Adjutant after Lord Sil?"

The marking on Sil's guardian ring popped into my mind. It resembled the Insignia that had glowed on my right hand the moment I became Klifford's Sovereign. Maybe that's why what Rust said had made sense to me somehow.

This *Adjutant*... Were they somehow connected to the origins of Sil's birth?

"I noticed...that you weren't surprised to hear me say the word *Adjutant*, Your Highness. Personally, I find the existence of Adjutants to be rather suspect, but do you not feel that way?" A smile formed on Rust's lips.

Urgh! I screwed up... Since I had a real Adjutant—Klifford—in my service, hearing the word from Rust didn't faze me at all. But it should have. Most people aren't even sure if Adjutants exist. That's just how elusive they are!

I should've been like, "Adjutant? What *are* you talking about, good sir?" If he'd asked me that question before I'd become a Sovereign, that's definitely how I would've reacted.

But wait... I can still salvage this.

I shifted my fan's position and snapped it open, bringing it close to my face so Rust couldn't see my expression very well. I took a breath to make sure I wouldn't put my foot in my mouth again. I needed to gain control and find out where they'd taken Sil!

I said in the calmest tone I could muster, "Well, yes, *Adjutants* are the things of *fairy tales* as far as I'm concerned. However, it would have been uncouth of me to shut down the conversation over such a detail. A princess must always pay heed to a story, no matter how nonsensical. And according to you, an Adjutant is targeting Lord Sil, no? So I took this claim seriously and asked you *why.*"

Okay, I dodged that bullet...I hope!

Taking Rust's lack of objection as a good sign, I repeated my question. "Why...why do you suppose an Adjutant is after Lord Sil?"

"Not sure."

Not sure? What do you mean you're not sure...?

"I already told you, I am not an anti-royalist collaborator. All I know is that an Adjutant is after Burks. And I know where he might be at present," he said, holding up two fingers. "Now, as for your question, why don't you ask the Adjutant who's after Burks personally?"

"Well...that would be ideal."

"You say it as if it were so easy." I sensed an insuppressible iciness in his tone. Yet his smile had not vanished. "Were you not aware? These Adjutants... They are a small warrior clan of many mysteries. Because they take on Sovereigns, those in power desire them. And in the end, this unlucky clan has been slipping out of existence. There are tales of one Adjutant slaying a hundred enemies to protect his Sovereign. They are incredibly difficult to defeat with regular battle tactics."

This was one of the legends passed down through generations to warn of the sheer power of Adjutants.

"If we hinder this Adjutant who's after Burks, that would make us his enemy. How exactly do you intend to take on an Adjutant in a fight, Your Highness?" Rust asked, taking the blue mask on the table into his hand. "What if, for example—"

Rust smiled and lunged at me. In the split second it happened, I noticed his expression completely clashed with his action. He had picked up his mask—not to put on but to use as a weapon to swiftly shove the mask's sharp edge in my face.

He was unarmed. He had no concealed weapons. But depending on how it was used...even a plain metal mask could cause some real damage.

I have to dodge it... The thought flashed in my brain. But my body didn't respond in time. It was just like that time I died in my past life... when the car was speeding right into me.

The mask turned weapon was coming close, right at eye level. It took only an instant...or maybe a few seconds...but it looked like slow motion to me.

Just like it did that fateful day...

But then...the mask lurched away from me. That was because someone had yanked me out of the way. As he held me protectively with his free arm, Klifford stood in front of me, his longsword drawn and pointed at Rust's neck. If Klifford shifted his stance even slightly, Rust's neck would bleed. It really was a close shave.

And the mask in Rust's hand was on a collision course with the spot where I had been sitting. It was so close... If I'd stayed seated, the sharp part of the mask probably would have struck me somewhere above my neck. All Rust needed to do was lean in and swiftly brandish the mask.

Neither Klifford nor Rust budged a millimeter. Klifford's calm voice broke the stalemate. "What shall I do with him?"

I swallowed hard. It was my job to pass judgment on him. I reached out and touched Klifford's sword arm. He glanced at me with just his eyes.

"I haven't finished speaking with him yet."

"Then...please finish your conversation in this position. If he makes any further suspicious movement, I'm cutting off his head."

I gave him a shallow nod. Then I looked at Rust, at the other end of Klifford's blade. "Do you have any intentions of doing so, Rust Byrne?"

"Of making any further suspicious movements? Er...no? I'd prefer to keep living, thank you."

"From the way you've been acting, that's hard to believe."

"Rebelling against the Crown is high treason, Your Highness... What will you do if it turns out I had no such intentions?"

"You...had no such intentions?"

"I was merely answering your question nonverbally, Your Highness. Shall I tell you what I was going to say after *What if, for example*? What if, for example...just like this...an Adjutant attacked you, Your Highness?"

As he said this, Rust dropped the blue mask in his hand. It landed on the table with a soft clink.

"I had no malicious intent. Perhaps your bodyguard can corroborate this."

"Klifford. What's your reading on the situation?"

"He…is not lying, Your Highness," Klifford answered, keeping his eyes locked on Rust. "Though whether he had malicious intent is somewhat irrelevant."

"I would have stopped myself from harming you at the last minute if necessary, Your Highness," Rust protested. "Besides, technically speaking, it was not *you* whom I was aiming for with my mask, Your Highness."

"It…wasn't *me*, you say?"

Um, if I'd stayed in that spot, I'm pretty sure your mask would have struck in the general vicinity of my face!

"Yes, Your Highness. I was aiming for the decoration in your hair—the Lieche orchids."

I touched my hand to the two Lieche orchids that were serving as a hair ornament. They were still there.

He was aiming for my hair accessory… Yeah, when everything was happening in slow motion, I did notice his mask was at the same level as my eyes. So that does check out. But still…

"Why would you aim for my hair decoration, of all things? Is it really that peculiar for a princess to wear real flowers in her hair?"

It was then that Rust looked at me for the first time… That's right. It was the *first time*.

My eyes finally met those amber orbs. The first time I saw Rust's bare face in the pleasaunce hall—and my shitty haunting memories came flooding back to me—I don't think I saw his eyes then. And yet, ever since we set foot in the garden, Rust avoided looking me in the eye. Even when I looked at him, he would only glance back before immediately averting his gaze. So our eyes had never met once.

Then, fast-forward to now. Rust maintained eye contact…and then shifted his gaze a bit. The amber orbs narrowed slightly. He was looking at...my Lieche hair decoration?

After a long pause, Rust murmured, "Idéalia..." His hoarse voice trailed off, not finishing his sentence.

"Idéalia?"

Was that...somebody's name?

"It's nothing—" Rust cut himself off there, cursing quietly and pressing a hand to the left side of his forehead where his scar was. And after only a few seconds, he lowered his hand and said, "Sorry. How disgraceful of me."

"That scar... You said you were born with it?"

The scar was a physical attribute he was born with—there may have been more to it, but nothing had made it into the published contents of the series.

"It is merely a scar. It should not hurt. It's a phantom pain—as you saw for yourself, it hurts at times."

"Does this *phantom pain* have a trigger?"

And is that trigger...the Lieche orchids?

When Rust first saw me in the pleasaunce hall, he'd frozen for a moment. Was it because I was wearing Lieche orchids in my hair? And was it also why he wouldn't look me in the eye after he removed his mask...?

Rust snickered creepily. "Yes, I suppose you could call it a trigger."

"Should I...remove these from my hair?"

"No," Rust answered sharply with a thin smirk. It was hard to determine whether he was being sincere. "Princess Octavia, you truly are a kind soul. Why should my phantom pain be of any concern to you? The reason I aimed for the flowers in your hair was because I did not wish to cause you any harm. However, have you already forgotten what I've done?"

"Why, no. You were answering my question nonverbally, yes?"

And even Klifford vouched that he had no malicious intent, so he was probably telling the truth. He probably meant to stop just short of touching me. But…one wrong move, and he would have fallen under suspicion of treason. So he must have had a very good reason for taking that action.

"Well, do you have your answer, then? To what I would do if an Adjutant attacked me?"

Rust chuckled deeply and shook his head. "I already had the answer from the very start. A fragile young lady like yourself is helpless. Even against someone who is neither an Adjutant nor genuinely trying to harm you."

Is that really true, though?

"……" I was silent while I considered it.

Though I hated to admit it, the implication behind his words was true. Klifford was the one who protected me. Had I been alone, I would not have been able to protect myself. So that meant…

"Are you implying…that was a lesson you wanted to teach me?"

No…a lesson he wanted me to learn firsthand?

"You want to rescue Burks—that is an admirable sentiment. But we're up against an Adjutant. Surely, we could not have a fragile princess such as yourself wield a sword, let alone fight with it. This would necessitate the burden of fighting falling onto someone else… However, I hope you haven't forgotten that, to most people, ordering them to fight an Adjutant is the same as ordering them to die. Then again, was it not the royal family who easily commanded their subjects to die for them while they stood safely on high ground?"

As Rust smoothly delivered his speech, a cool smile formed on his face—a smile of contempt. It was viscerally clear that he felt disgust toward Esfia's royal family and its princess—me. It was a disgust that ran deep.

This time, Rust had sided against the traitors. And when he'd lunged at me with the mask, that was likely mere posturing. But all of this meant he was still as he was written in the books… He was an anti-royalist.

"You've made your case quite clear… I will pardon your transgression."

"You are the same princess who spared the life of a soldier who threw a sword at her by accident. I knew you would pardon my actions as well."

"Tell me where Lord Sil is being kept—that is my condition for your pardon."

The issue at hand was Sil's abduction, and Rust was our only connection to finding him. So Rust's punishment was not a priority.

"And I *shall* tell you, Your Highness...*if* you show me you are sincere."

"If I show you...I am sincere?"

"Do you have the grit to commit the foolish act of going personally to find Sil Burks? If so, then I shall yield to you out of respect and accompany you."

I was about to rush into a place I knew was dangerous to rescue Sil—that was the definition of a foolish act. But I couldn't ask Uncle Dearest and his men for help. They would definitely stop me from going. But if I didn't go personally, Rust wouldn't divulge a word of what he knew. And he certainly wouldn't escort anyone else there.

Then what would happen to Sil?

Time was ticking. If I went personally to rescue Sil, and if it looked like I was indeed being led into a trap, that wouldn't shake my conviction. I'd have no regrets, either.

But...what if I had a chance of winning? Even if we're up against an Adjutant, the playing field is still even. And the key to victory stood right beside me.

"Klifford," I called out to my armed bodyguard without hesitation. I didn't stand a chance against an Adjutant. And there was only one person who could fight in my place... "Do you think you could win in a fight against the Adjutant who's after Lord Sil?"

Klifford's lips softened slightly into a smile. "If you *command* it of me, Your Highness."

Fight Adjutant with Adjutant—the clear and simple solution. But I almost second-guessed myself, wondering if this was truly for the best. Commanding a man to fight an Adjutant was the same as demanding

that he die. Though I figured Klifford would find a way out of dying...
But what if he didn't?

"Your Highness... Do you not trust me?" Klifford's voice fell softly
from above like rain, washing away my worries.

"No... I do trust you." I raised my head, overwhelmed. His indigo
eyes entered my field of view.

"Then please, give me your command."

"If you must fight an Adjutant...promise me you will win."

"Yes. I promise."

*There. Now everything is set in stone. Klifford gave me his word—all
I can do is trust him.*

I accepted Rust's proposal. "Yes, I'd love to commit a foolish act.
You'll take me there, I hope?"

36

With Blackfeather opened in my right hand, a genial smile bloomed
on my face. On my left side walked Rust, in his mask. This was so we
could locate Sil, swiftly and secretly—it was vital that nobody thought
anything about us was amiss until we got to him. We wanted to avoid
being approached and stopped for conversation.

To the rest of the guests, we appeared to be a man and woman who'd
met in the pleasaunce hall and hit it off. The only difference was that
we had a bodyguard in our company.

Who's that masked man with the princess? The other party guests
couldn't help but brim with curiosity. But it was better that than them
knowing our true purpose.

The farther we walked, the louder the orchestra's music grew. Paradise in the Sky was perched just above the foot of the mountains. Even
though it was an hour away from the castle by carriage, its elevated

location was one of the many reasons it was a prized venue for junior balls.

Esfia's people loved high places—because the Sky God was the most popular deity in Esfian tradition. The closer one was to the sky, the more divine. "Paradise in the Sky" was more than just a name.

But if you left the venue grounds, the road to the nearest town was shrouded gloomily in overgrown trees. It was the ideal route for the traitors to sneak in—a fact that did us little good to know now.

I even started to wonder if maybe Sil wasn't even in Paradise in the Sky anymore. But Rust, who knew where Sil was, wasn't taking us outside. We were supposed to wait in the garden for my safety, so when Rust suddenly tried to take the princess of Esfia away, it was no wonder the garden guards tried to stop him.

So I said that I just remembered there was a party guest I was supposed to meet with. My story gave them a little push—steamrolled them, rather, by the power of Princess Privilege—and they let us leave the garden. But one vital piece of information—our destination—was still unknown to me.

Rust promised he would tell me where Sil was if I committed a foolish act. But instead of *telling* me where Sil was, he was *taking* me there. It didn't look like Rust was headed toward the venue entrance.

So in other words, Sil was still somewhere inside Paradise in the Sky.

I kept step with Rust, exuding the aura that I was enjoying myself at the junior ball. We slipped through the corridor and passed right through the main hall without stopping. We turned a corner and entered a narrow passageway. There were noticeably far fewer party guests now. Then we climbed the stairs. And at their top...

I pursed my lips and glanced sideways up at Rust, walking beside me.

Sensing my penetrating gaze, Rust said, "Fear not, Princess, I will take you to Burks as promised." His mask hid his expression, but he was trying not to look at the Lieche orchids in my hair.

"At the top of these stairs…," I began, "there can only be one thing."

"Yes, it remains here *because* Paradise in the Sky used to house the royal family. It is a room of great significance to Your Highness, I presume?"

"Yes… It's the Sky Chamber."

The Sky Chamber was the only room that could possibly be at the top of these stairs. After passing through a circular corridor, we finally arrived at its door. By its nature, it was closed. It would have been so regardless of a junior ball being held.

The Sky Chamber was primarily blue, with the morning, noon, and night skies painted on its walls and ceiling. The biggest spectacle of all was the night sky—it was darkened like a planetarium, with stars twinkling above.

The room contained one throne. And no wonder it did—Paradise in the Sky used to belong to Esfia's royal family. Moreover, King Eus was the one who had let it go. It was built in the Sky God's name and had served as the royal family's villa. King Eus in particular favored living here, rather than in the royal castle. And even though he loved it dearly, he'd bestowed the land—building and all—to his vassal as a reward the year before he died.

—With the addendums: "*Paradise in the Sky cannot be returned to the royal family*" and "*The throne room must remain untouched.*"

Part of the reason behind this was so the next king couldn't be all crazy like, "Nah, that didn't count! Undo! Gimme back!" The other reason was because King Eus loved the throne room in his villa most of all—at least, that's how the story was interpreted.

And now, centuries later, the royal villa had metamorphosed into a rental hall. Its current owner was my (male) mother, Lord Edgar, and the company he was deeply tied to. Since it held nothing but the finest furnishings, it was dubbed Paradise in the Sky. Its name encompassed the height at which the building stood—and the building itself.

Even as a rental hall, the building's historical value had not disappeared. King Eus's name was magnificent—even in its royal villa days, the throne room was called the Sky Chamber—and still today it was carefully preserved to exist as it did in the past.

Ordinarily, the Sky Chamber's door would be locked, with a guard stationed both inside and out. Once you entered it, your only way out was through the circular corridor. This meant, if you weren't careful, you could get trapped inside. If, say, you were surrounded by a sizeable platoon…it was curtains for you.

So what was Sil doing in there?

"Are you sure that Lord Sil is in the Sky Chamber?"

"Yes. Burks is indeed in *the Sky Chamber.*"

If Sil was in the Sky Chamber, the guard should have informed someone. And there wasn't even a place for a person to hide, besides.

"Your Highness, have you never set foot in the Sky Chamber before?"

"Just once."

That's how I knew what it looked like inside. One time, I invited Alec to join me on a little royal expedition. Since Alec loved the Great Corridor so much, I thought he might be interested in the Sky Chamber as well. But as it turned out, he didn't really want to go in. He only went along so he wouldn't hurt my feelings…

As soon as we stepped inside, Alec's face drained of color, and he became ill.

"Just once, you say?" Rust looked at me. "Why only once?"

That was because—

"Dear Sister, please…please don't go in the Sky Chamber."

Alec had suddenly become ill, so I'd taken him out of the beautiful blue room. And just as I was about to leave his side, he grabbed my arm and begged, his head hanging.

It concerned me. "Alec? What's the matter?"

"Please…please forgive me, dear Sister. That was…quite a silly thing I just said." Alec looked up and quickly retracted his request.

But for some reason, I felt terribly anxious—like I might burst into tears any minute. I wasn't so fascinated by the Sky Chamber that Alec's pitiful face wouldn't stop me from going inside.

That was why I'd only entered the Sky Chamber once.

"Are you suggesting that royalty has some sort of duty to visit the Sky Chamber regularly?" I asked.

"No… But I do wonder what made King Eus release ownership of his villa. As his descendent, what do you think, Your Highness?"

"Is it…really that important anymore?"

"No?" Rust smiled…but only in his lips. That smile vanished quickly.

We walked the circular corridor until the door to the Sky Chamber was in sight. However…

There's not a single guard.

This couldn't have been sanctioned by the venue staff. Something was afoot in the Sky Chamber.

"Well, well, well. That's saved us the trouble of fighting off the guards, eh?" Rust joked.

"Are you implying…that the situation isn't as you imagined it would be?"

"I imagined there would be a guard stationed at the door. A *fake* guard, that is."

So since the fake guard in question isn't here…the enemy Adjutant's plan hit a snag?

"Burks probably fought back. Either way, we shall find out when we open this door." The blue double doors stood invitingly before Rust's extended arm.

An image of Alec's face popped into my mind. He would probably be upset if he found out I went into the Sky Chamber while he was gone. And that I was jumping into danger of my own volition.

But…Sil's life is on the line. And I'm not jumping in alone, besides. "Klifford," I called.

"Aye."

He knew my command without me saying it. Klifford stood before the doors and pushed them open without hesitation. Barely a second later, his longsword was drawn.

The sound of clashing swords rang out, much louder than they had back in the garden. And charging at Klifford from inside the Sky Chamber was—

"Lord Derek?" I gasped dumbfoundedly.

Derek looked my way...then his gaze returned to Klifford. Then with a sigh, he lowered his sword.

"Princess Octavia... What are you doing here?" he asked, quizzically furrowing his brow.

Wh-what?

"Did someone...do something to you?" he asked, worried this time.

He wouldn't... Does he notice, under all the makeup, the redness in my eyes from crying? No way... I checked myself in the mirror. And the Paradise in the Sky staff's makeup skills were perfect—they were that of an artist. Derek's eyes are just abnormally sharp! His perception—his sharpness!—comes straight from Uncle Dearest.

But...I didn't want anyone to find out I was crying. "I put living flowers in my hair for a change of mood. Then I had my makeup retouched to match—that's all."

Derek blinked a couple times and opened his mouth to say something...then he thought better of it and closed it briefly before saying, "Lieche orchids, moreover? Well, that's quite like you, Princess Octavia, I'll say as much."

"Lord Derek. Isn't Lord Sil's safety a more pressing matter than my hair?"

"I did instruct the guard who delivered the message to me about Sil to deliver a message to you—"

"I suppose there was a missed connection."

"Yes...I suppose there was." Derek sighed deeply.

"And what did this message entail?"

"Please, stay where you are."

In other words, *"Be a good girl and stay put."* Well, even if I had received that message, I still would've come here.

In the beautiful blue room, there stood one throne. And two other guests besides Derek—the aforementioned fake guards—were lying unconscious.

Derek explained to me that he'd come to the Sky Chamber to look for Sil when the fake guards attacked him. He only had the upper hand because he'd already had his suspicions about them earlier. They were both dressed in venue guards' uniforms. And their longswords bore the distinctive venue markings as well.

Yet Derek still suspected them. He had two reasons. First, one of the guards had triple piercings in his left ear. It was almost as if he'd removed his Khangenan hoop earrings in haste. As was the case at the royal castle, in important places like the Sky Chamber, foreigners were never employed as guards. While there were exceptions when such foreigners were under Esfia's jurisdiction…if he had ear piercings—a sign that he was a Khangenan through and through—the chances of him being a real guard were very slim indeed. And second, another guard had been talking to this Khangenan guard, as if nothing was amiss.

We walked into the chamber where the two fallen men lay.

"As for those fake guards, neither of them talked. Aside from being ordered not to let anyone pass, it's likely they weren't given any information." Derek hovered over them regally, longsword in hand. From the way he was glaring down at them, it looked like he would strike them any minute.

Listening to Derek's story, some underlying suspicions I'd had of him slowly surfaced. While I did believe Derek was on Sil's side, the fact that I'd bumped into him in the Sky Chamber in pursuit of Sil—when Sil himself was still missing—had given me cause to suspect him.

Then there was the fact that Derek did not lower his sword, even when it was revealed that the intruder was Klifford.

Wait…huh? Let's say Derek was looking for Sil because his intentions were pure… How was he able to make it into the Sky Chamber?

"By the way, who is that with you?" Derek suddenly asked. He wasn't wearing his nobleman's smile—probably because he didn't deem it necessary. He was staring at Rust, the masked man, without a hint of a grin.

"You know about the plan to catch the anti-royalists at this junior ball? Well, he helped Countess Rosa carry it out."

"Oh, right. My father was rather enthusiastic about something—is that what it was?"

Wait... Did Uncle Dearest not tell Derek about the plan? "Do you mean to say that Duke Nightfellow did not inform you of the plan?" Was Derek actually in the dark with me all this time?

"Well, he did tell me to stay out of the way."

So that's all it took for him to get it...

"Sometimes it's best that those involved not know all the details. Now, why is it that someone under Countess Reddington's employ is accompanying you away from the party, Princess Octavia? I doubt Countess Reddington sanctioned it—and I would love to know the reason why he keeps his face masked."

Before I could answer, Rust said, "To answer your first question, son of Duke Nightfellow, it is because I have a clue on Sil Burks's whereabouts. As for the second, I do not wish for the Adjutant who's after Burks to see my face."

".......Adjutant?" Derek's gaze grew grim.

Butting into their conversation, I announced, "Rust Byrne, I am committing a foolish act." Since Derek was the one inside the Sky Chamber, I found it necessary to hear his side of the story first. And even though he hadn't finished yet, there was something I needed Rust to confirm to me first.

"Yes. You are showing me how sincere you are this very minute."

"In exchange...you promised to take me to Lord Sil. You've taken me here, to the Sky Chamber. Yet I do not see Lord Sil."

There weren't even any traces of Sil ever having been here. That wasn't part of the deal.

"Where is Sil?"

Without moving a muscle, Rust slowly said, "In the Sky Chamber. You suspected as much—is that not why you came here, son of Duke Nightfellow?"

Another Alexis

I have this dream—a dream where I kill my sister.

In this dream, my sister is not the girl with silvery hair and gentle aquamarine eyes that I know.

Her hair is silver, but of a different shade. Her eyes are a different color, too—they're green.

But I know she is my sister.

She is the queen.

And...I kill the queen.

As she lies there, her flame of life fading out from a mortal wound I—her younger brother—inflicted upon her, she smiles faintly. She gently presses a hand to her little brother's cheek as if to say "*Well done.*"

And that...is her final moment.

Her hand slips to the ground, all strength gone.

"Sister..."

I shake her corpse. But it only grows colder in reply. My sister is gone.

"Sister!"

But her silvery hair only tangles beneath the crown she had to wear because of me.

"Tell me why...! Why me?"

I keep shaking her. Even though I know the action is meaningless.

It's almost as if I believe that, in doing so, the life I stole from her will return.

But no miracle comes to us.

It *never* has—

I choke out a sob, embracing her corpse and burying my face in her hair.

"Congratulations, Your Highness... No, Your Majesty." A man speaks to me as I shake with tears. From the state of his clothes, drenched with red, one could imagine the number of lives he'd taken before arriving here.

But I am in the same state. I am covered in my sister's blood—defiling the blue walls of the room she loved so much.

"No...I will *not* become king."

"You mean to disregard your sister's wish?"

I glare at the man. He lowers his bloodstained sword and bows to me.

"Don't..."

"A new king is born. What a blessed day...King Eus."

"Shut up...shut up, Alderton!"

King Eus—the same name as the great king of yore—that is the name I am called in this dream.

"A blessed day? Like hell it is...," I spit. "I killed my sister—what could possibly be blessed about that?!"

How dare he say it's blessed.

"*Because* you killed your sister. It was a duty you had to perform. Your sister's enthronement plunged this kingdom into disarray—you must be the next king."

So I can make things right...he means to say.

"But I don't want...!" I clench my teeth.

I know what my sister's wishes were. She was the queen to the very end. A queen who loved her kingdom...her subjects...

But...

I feel something dark crawling up from below.

How could I possibly love this kingdom? Someone like me. A neglected prince.

This kingdom...that killed my sister...my one and only refuge...

This is madness...

I look down at the body in my arms...my sister's body...its veins now bloodless.

A drop of blood adorns her face, now ashen white.

I want to wipe it clean. I wipe it with my fingertip. But the blood does not vanish—it only stains her face more. That is because my hands are already stained with blood.

My face twitches.

I loved to read... I would shut myself in the library for hours, forgetting to eat or sleep. My sister yelled at me often for this.

I'd embraced the ideal world from my books—and I was mocked for being fanciful. For having such fanciful notions that human beings could come to understand each other by talking things through. That they could make peace with each other.

War... I'd hated it. And blood... I'd hated the color of blood.

So I had hated my sister's Adjutant. He made a living from war.

And yet now...war...and the red stain of blood... All of it is on my hands.

"Sister..."

Why did all of this happen...?

Why did I have to kill my sister?

I'd had a bright future ahead... It was supposed to be mine.

My sister would become queen, and I would serve as her vassal. I wanted to support her, as long as she loved Esfia.

I can picture it all so clearly.

Me, crowned King Eus, before my joyous subjects.

At my sister's enthronement, the people of Esfia had cheered in celebration. And those same subjects—the subjects who sang her praises—
turned their backs on her.

It was as if they were opposed to her rule as queen from the very
start.

The natural disasters were a manifestation of the Sky God's wrath.
Everything wrong with the world would be set right with the queen's
death.

Swept away—manipulated—on a wave of agitation, Esfia's people
lost faith in the queen who had always loved them so dearly...and they
took up arms against her. That's how it came to this... This was
inevitable...

Those fools... No matter how much she showered them with love,
they were still fools. Fools who would never realize how foolish they
were. And there was no use in trying to talk things over with fools—
not when they were "puppets made to dance."

Did such fools even deserve to live?

"...fall to ruin."

My voice cracks as my emotions spill out of me.

Curse Esfia... It can fall to ruin.

No...

I will bring it to ruin.

I swear it.

Alexis held his head in his hands, shaking it over and over. His face
was twisted with pain.

This was the first time he'd had this dream in the middle of the day.

He felt sick...terribly sick. He always felt overwhelmingly parched
after having that dream.

He reached for the water jug and gulped it straight from the
spout, abandoning proper decorum. The water wet his throat—and

an illusion in which his thirst was quenched took hold of him slightly. His was a thirst that water could not quench.

With the water jug in one hand, he wiped his mouth with the other.

"Sister…" Before he realized it, Alexis was calling out to his sister just as he had in the dream.

If he could only see his sister, Octavia…his thirst would be quenched.

In his dream, he killed his sister. In the dream, she ceased to exist beyond that point.

But in the real world, Alexis's sister was alive. She existed.

The thirst he felt now was his dream-self…parched from the grief of loss.

Why did I have such a dream…? he asked himself.

At first, he was confused. He'd never once thought about harming his sister. The fact that he seemed to be King Eus in his dream only furthered his confusion.

The dream itself was filled with inconsistencies. If he believed his dream was true, that was the moment King Eus came into being. He killed his sister to become king. And by his side, there was a man named Alderton… It was a cunning mix of truth and falsehood.

In reality, King Eus had succeeded his father directly. And Count Alderton had led an uprising against him.

Count Alderton led a house of mighty warriors. He had been relatively young and dissatisfied with King Eus barely a moment after he was enthroned. A clash of opinions led to a drawing of weapons and an uprising against his king.

But the uprising had ended in failure.

King Eus pardoned Count Alderton. While he did send him away from his inner circle, he did not kill the traitor. And the count's house still existed to this very day—one of its members was Octavia's bodyguard: Klifford Alderton.

Overcome with pain, Alexis roughly slammed down the water jug. The ceramic jug clanged loudly.

—Dream and reality…were completely different from one another.

First and foremost, Esfia did not fall to ruin. The opposite, in fact—
King Eus was the one who brought prosperity to Esfia.

But in his dream, King Eus despised his kingdom.

What if this dream wasn't a dream? What if it was Esfia's true history?

Well, that would be ridiculous—Esfia *didn't* fall to ruin.

Esfia's true history was exactly the opposite.

In the history books, King Eus was written as a model king who lived to serve his kingdom. His policies spoke for themselves. So it could not be said that the dream told what really had happened. No matter how painfully raw the fragments of the dream felt…the dream in which he himself was King Eus.

But the King Eus of the dream and Alexis did have some things in common. The sister in the dream and his sister, Octavia. Alexis's position in life also closely resembled King Eus's in the dream. King Eus was also the black sheep of the royal family. His sister was the one person who called him family. And yet, by his own hand…

"I will not become like King Eus…," he murmured, convincing himself of it. I will never make a blunder like I did in the dream—like King Eus did.

The thirst would not be quenched…

He had to finish his mission and return to the castle as soon as possible.

Alexis walked over to the windowsill of his room at the inn. According to plan, they would start camping outdoors on the morrow. It was a suggestion Alexis himself had made, in hopes of arriving at their destination as soon as possible.

Their destination—Turchen.

In his dream, as King Eus, he had been there before. To Turchen, the kingdom that had become a land of carnage from the brutal war against Khangena. Unable to end the war, they'd signed an accord with Khangena.

And even in the fragmented dream, this much was clear: King Eus did not fight against Khangena for Esfia's sake. Not in the least.

He fought to kill his sister's Adjutant.

And naturally, Alexis's reason for going to Turchen now was different.

"Go to Turchen to spy for me. Report back to me everything you see and hear there…" The king paused. "Alexis."

"You want me to go? Not Sirius?"

"Sirius would stand out too much."

"But Fath—Your Majesty—"

"I'm sending you on this mission for Octavia's sake as well."

"Then…I accept the mission, Your Majesty."

He accepted the mission because it was the first time his father had personally commanded an important task of him. He was so honored. He wanted to make his father proud. And if this mission would help his sister, what further motivation did he need? If he produced good results…then maybe the way his father looked at him would change.

But another part of Alexis—the part of him influenced by King Eus in his dream—whispered in his ear: *Does your father have ulterior motives?*

Maybe he should have said no. Only now, when he was far away from the castle, did his worries grow.

From the windowsill on which he leaned, he could see the stars twinkling in the night sky. This sky merged with the sky from his dream—a fake sky, painted blue.

Alexis closed his eyes. "I know why I'm worried… It's because my sister is at Paradise in the Sky right now."

He knew Octavia would be at the junior ball right about then. It was to be held at Paradise in the Sky. When it came to hosting junior balls for the aristocracy, nothing was more suitable. It was well guarded, too.

If his sister wanted to go, then he had no clear reason to stop her. If not for his mission, he would have wanted to be her escort. He was no longer a child under his big sister's protective wing. He was to protect *her* now.

I want to keep her away from that room—so she won't enter it even by accident.

That room that they once visited together...

Once was more than enough. If the events of that dream lie within that room—then I never want to go there. And I don't want Octavia to go there, either.

He knew that he only felt that way because of the dream... He knew that.

But even if nothing bad was happening to her, he felt so restless... stuck alone in the inn.

Alexis opened his eyes when there was a knock at his door. "Who's there?" he demanded.

"Randal."

The voice did indeed belong to Randal, a knight he had employed. There was nothing unnatural or irregular about his speech. After determining it was safe, Alexis let him in.

"Enter."

"Pardon me, Your Highness. I've come with the report."

"Speak."

Randal closed the door behind him and said, "I did not detect any suspicious behavior from any of the men His Majesty chose to accompany you on this mission. While there were several cads at this inn who had insolent thoughts upon seeing you, Your Highness, they have all been disposed of."

"By insolent thoughts...you mean, they recognized me as the prince?"

Randal stammered awkwardly. "Er, no... Your identity as the second prince of Esfia remains hidden."

"Very well. You may go now."

It was vexing, knowing just how much a certain sort of man admired his physique—boyish though it still was. It was quite the ordeal just choosing his own subordinates. For his closest associates, he preferred men who were gifted—and who didn't look at him lustfully. And Randal met these two requirements. He was common-born, though—that was one problem.

But when he prioritized the former two requirements over a man's social status, commoners were easier to keep, since there were so many of them.

At his core, Alexis did not value commoners. This wasn't because of the lessons he received as royalty. His elder brother, Sirius, thought of commoners differently from him, as did his father, who had married Edgar—a former merchant.

Octavia differed, too—she longed to mingle among the commoners. Sometimes Alexis thought that she felt suffocated by her station in life.

Alexis alone felt differently…and he knew his dreams were the reason why.

King Eus resented his kingdom—despised it, even. The majority of his subjects were commoners. It was bands of commoners who had been easily manipulated into revolting. It was commoners who had conveniently forgotten the harm they'd done.

How could he possibly trust them? How could he cherish them?

Did fools need rights? No—they didn't.

And were there exceptions among the commoners? Alexis already knew the answer to that. So his primal instincts remained steadfast. He would make an exception with those exceptional people and interact with them accordingly.

"Prince Alexis, shall I continue my watch?"

"Yes."

"Understood." Randal tucked in his chin, bowed, and left the room. Randal knew when to stop asking questions.

Left alone in his room, Alexis murmured in a voice only he could hear. "I wonder…if my father is trying to kill me." It was suspicious that the king assigned so many men of dubious trustworthiness to accompany the second prince of Esfia on a mission. It was as if he was afraid of something.

In Alexis's dream, he was King Eus. So he was unable to see his own face. But at times, Alexis did catch a glimpse of King Eus's face in a broken mirror in the dream. He had golden hair and amber eyes. He did not resemble Alexis, his father, or Sirius or Octavia, either.

But there was one thing that was familiar—the light in his eyes. It gave Alexis a sense of déjà vu. He wasn't sure where he'd seen it before. But when he sat down to dinner later that night, the indifferent look in his father's eyes made his heart stop with a sudden realization. It was indifference—a look his father had given him so many times. Alexis's father was indifferent to him.

It was because his father had looked at him indifferently so often… that when he gave him *that other look* instead, it struck him all the more. It was a look as if he had something hidden deep inside…something that failed to subside completely…and it had burst to the surface.

"It's hatred."

It didn't make sense. He knew the circumstances of his birth. Was it because he was an unwanted child? Was that enough to deserve hatred?

"But…Father…," he called out to his father, who was not there. "If you must hate someone—shouldn't it also be my birth mother?"

If he hated both mother and child, Alexis could understand that. But…that wasn't the case.

At the very least, his father did not hate the woman he'd shared a night with. The look in his eyes seemed to say that he thought of Alexis's birth mother as a victim.

Alexis never met his birth mother. But he had seen her before. He'd heard her voice. It was a secret nobody knew.

"Your Majesty, please forgive the intrusion. The sight of me must cause you much discomfort."

"I feel no discomfort in seeing you… I should have been more careful that night. If anyone should apologize, it is I."

When Alexis heard some of the castle staff whispering that his birth mother had secretly come to the castle to visit, he sneaked out of his room to catch a glimpse of her. That was when he overheard the conversation between the two of them.

There was not a hint of resentment in the air. The relationship between his birth parents was not at all bad. Alexis felt that this should please him...but it didn't.

If his father accepted his mother—then why was *he* neglected? Hated, even.

"...in front of......grave...would...acceptable?"

"That's... Edgar would..."

Alexis covered his ears to shut out the fragments of their conversation, turned his back on his parents, and fled to the Great Corridor. The Great Corridor was a favorite place of his—of Alexis's, that is. In his dream, King Eus detested it.

Using the ornamental carvings as footholds, Alec climbed up one of the pillars of the Great Corridor and hid himself in one of the depressions of the room, when he heard a voice from below.

"Alec, I thought that was you. Your bodyguard is looking for you."

Being fourteen years old now, Alec was too big to fully hide himself there anymore. But he was smaller back then, so he could.

"Big sister...?" He peeked out from his hiding nook. And there was his beloved big sister—Octavia—looking up at him.

"Go back to your room, okay?"

"No..." He sulked, knowing Octavia would let him get away with it.

His sister looked perplexed, but only for a moment. "Okay, how would you like to come to my room, then?"

"Your room...?"

"That's right. We could talk, and you could sleep in my bed with me tonight. Isn't that a great idea? So come down, Alec. Please?"

"Okay..."

He started to climb down, but he made an uncharacteristic mistake. He lost his footing and fell—not a long way, but he fell all the same.

But it wasn't the cold, hard floor that broke his fall. It was something soft and warm. His big sister was beneath him, like a mattress.

He felt an icy chill. "Oh! Dear Sister?!"

Octavia half sat up and smiled. "You gave me a scare. Good thing I caught you in time. Are you okay, Alec?"

Overcome with relief, all Alec could do was nod silently in reply.

"Please, don't look so sad. I'm fine."

"I'm sorry..."

"Alec?"

"Sister...don't you hate me?" He wouldn't look up. His father's eyes, brimming with hate, were in his mind. Those eyes, filled with the same hatred of King Eus—of himself in the dream.

"Alec, you're a very smart boy, but you can be so foolish over the strangest things. I would never hate you, Alec. You're my baby brother, and I love you. You're the only one who..."

He slowly looked up, anxious to hear the rest of her sentence. But she only smiled gently and patted his head. He felt his face scrunch up with tears when she did that.

"I love you, too, Sister... I would never hate you...*never*. You mean everything to me..."

Even though his father hated him, his big sister, Octavia, showered him with an almost alarming amount of love and affection.

A dream where King Eus kills his sister—

I won't let the mistakes in the dream be repeated.

Until the bitter end, King Eus put the wishes of his sister over his own, and he granted them.

But his sister—she rejected his wish for her to keep living.

This was all to entrust the kingdom to her little brother. But the little brother in question did not want that one bit.

King Eus should have prioritized his own wish.

When Alec closed his eyes, the beautiful blue—so unbefitting of a tragedy—surfaced in his memory on a current of pain.

The place that set the stage in his dream was now called Paradise in the Sky, and it was out of the royal family's hands. It was formerly the villa of Esfia's royal family.

—In the true *Sky Chamber*.

37

It seemed as though Rust was seeking an answer of agreement from Derek, but he quickly turned to me instead and said, "On that note, Princess Octavia, do you give me permission to investigate this room—that is, to not leave it *untouched*?"

Due to the silvery-blue mask obscuring his face, I could not tell what exactly was on his mind. Ever since we arrived, my patience was wearing thinner and thinner. I opened Blackfeather to soothe my nerves. In times like this, nothing beats floof! *Okay... I feel better now.*

"To what, exactly, are you referring?"

"'*The throne room must remain untouched*'—King Eus's decree has been honored for centuries since he bequeathed the villa to his vassal. My actions would be in direct defiance of this. Now, were I an unscrupulous rogue who wished to rebel against the crown, it would not concern me—but I am no traitor. Violating a royal decree is a terrifying notion to me."

Rust—an anti-royalist—is terrified of rebelling? "And...your point is?"

Even with his mask, I could clearly see the edges of Rust's mouth turn sharply upward. "My point is...I must at least have your permission, Princess Octavia. Otherwise, His Majesty the King or Queen Edgar—the present owner of Paradise in the Sky—would punish me in King Eus's stead."

"Are you trying to say that His Majesty and his husband would oppose your actions, even if they led to the rescue of Lord Sil?"

"If history is any indicator, then it is certain. Take, for example, the time when the former king was alive, and King Enoch was crown prince—"

Rust's smile vanished. He extended an arm toward the Sky Chamber and said, "—and he entered this room in secret. That act alone earned him a severe punishment, I hear."

Just coming in here got him punished? Well, I doubt that would happen to me... No, yeah, when Alec and I came here, I think I got permission. I didn't exactly come here "in secret."

"I'll ask again, Your Highness. Will you grant me permission to violate a royal decree?"

One thing was clear: Rust was not afraid of violating a royal decree. Which made his reasons for making a point to ask me for permission all the more perplexing.

"I suppose this request would fall under the certain *grit* you asked of me?"

This would be a foolish act on top of a foolish act.

"Princess Octavia." Derek, who had been watching over the exchange with a steadfast look of scorn on his face, called my name. He said nothing more—he merely shook his head left to right. I figured he wanted me to refuse Rust's request.

I tightened my grip on Blackfeather. And once more, I took a look around the Sky Chamber. The color scheme inside was blue. The room's sonority was tangible, what with the crest of the Esfian royal family painted upon it. And with the lone throne sitting in the middle—it was excessively minimalistic.

In addition to the two unconscious fake guards, the room held Klifford, its prior visitor Derek, our guide Rust, and me. While we were technically here to look for someone, there was no such place for a person to hide here. But if Rust wasn't lying when he told me that Sil was inside the Sky Chamber...

That must mean this room contained something yet unknown to me.

"The throne room must remain untouched—"

Opening up the throne room was probably an unwelcome occurrence to the royal family. And as Esfia's princess, I probably shouldn't let it happen. Even Derek, who wanted to find Sil just as badly as I did, was against it—that's just how sacred the decree was.

But—

I closed my fan and looked directly at Rust. "I give my permission."

When Sil's life was hanging in the balance, the choice was obvious! If I dispiritedly pulled away now, what kind of woman would I be? Even if it turned out that nothing bad happened to Sil, I'd never forgive myself for not acting.

"Without my permission, you're in no mood to do anything. Is that not so, Rust Byrne? Everything you do in this room comes with the express permission of myself—Esfia's princess. I shall take full responsibility. Will that suffice?"

There! I dare you to make a complaint now.

"Well, what are you waiting for? Go violate a royal decree."

Under my encouragement, Rust gave a grand bow. "Well, then…as you wish, Princess Octavia." He looked up and smiled. Then he set off toward the one piece of furniture in the Sky Chamber: the throne.

The throne was shining with gold—and not just the color. Its back, its armrests, its legs… Every part of it was made of gold. It looked uncomfortable to sit on, but it was a luxury that evoked the opulence of King Eus's era. You might say the room's minimalism was more than made up for by the throne.

So. The thing about gold is…*it's much heavier than it looks*!

In terms of gold bars, the Sky Chamber throne was easily made of ten to twenty. So it wasn't an easy piece of furniture to move…to the untrained eye. If you knew of its existence in advance, or if you meticulously searched the throne all over, you would find a device in a part of the chair where you wouldn't think to look. A device that Rust activated handily now.

And the throne—which would ordinarily take a team to move—slid aside as if it were alive. As it moved, a unique noise rang throughout the room. It resembled the sound the gears made when the gate was raised for Alec's departure. Maybe it used the same mechanism.

Is this why you have to walk in a big circle to get into the Sky Chamber?

The noise stopped. The throne—was gone.

Where the throne once stood, there was a hollow space. Alec's face popped into my memory—sickened and begging me not to go into the Sky Chamber.

A downward staircase came into view—where it led was a mystery. I associated it with a secret passageway for royalty. If you casually set foot on such a staircase, you would lose all sense of direction in no time. For the passageway was like an ant's nest—branching haphazardly into many tunnels. It was the sort of place where what seemed to be an important room would be a dead end. Or, worst case scenario, you'd meet your doom.

It's that old story—you build a secret escape tunnel to keep you safe in an emergency, but bandits wind up using it to sneak in instead. And as the years pass, the whole thing just gets more and more complicated.

I swallowed hard.

Paradise in the Sky used to serve as a royal villa. What's more, it was the place that King Eus—a man who was both greatly revered and reviled—had loved very much. A secret passageway hidden behind its walls was not at all surprising.

So in other words...this labyrinth itself is also a part of it?

"Can you really guide us beyond this point? It seems that one would need a map to navigate through here."

"Oh, I do have a map. Right here," Rust said, pointing at his head. "Remember what I said? If you come of your own volition, I would accompany you and guide you to Burks."

"Well... Now I see why I needed you to guide me."

No matter how heavily guarded a person was, without the required knowledge, they could never find the hidden entrance—nor the secret passageway behind it. If anything, the Sky Chamber was actually a sanctuary of sorts. The sort of place you'd arrive at after a lifetime of searching. If you didn't know what to look for, you wouldn't know it even existed.

"I suppose the throne is a sort of door? What with the room being closed off and also guarded, I doubt anyone who did enter the room would even bother touching the throne."

"And even if someone did touch the throne, it would not move so easily, I figure. Not unless that somebody knew how its mechanism worked."

"And even if they did know about the mechanism, that alone would not be enough. Without knowing the correct way to do so, entering this room is already a difficult task. You'd have to draw up a plan like the traitors did. If you only wished to enter this room—the higher one's status, the easier everything would become," Rust added.

Just knowing about the throne's mechanism or entering the Sky Chamber was not enough. Did my father come to this secret passageway when he was the crown prince? Does that mean he also knows about this entrance?

Whoa... Hold up. Why was this secret passageway even left intact in the first place?

The secret passageway was probably in place ever since King Eus's reign. That's why Eus didn't want anyone coming in here—he didn't want anyone to find the entrance, right?

But why did he give this place away to his vassal? He could have sealed off the entrance completely without saying a word. Surely it would have been better to keep Paradise in the Sky in the family.

And sure enough, since the secret passageway and its entrance were left intact all this time, the Adjutant who's after Sil was able to use it...

Then...why did the Adjutant...?

"But my... How strange it is," Rust murmured, looking down at the entrance he had exposed. Something in his tone sounded a little disappointed to me.

"Were your hopes shattered, perhaps?"

"Oh, I had no hopes at all. It's that sound... It surely alerted the intruder ahead of us that somebody else has tripped the mechanism. I figured several men would be on their way to intercept us this very minute. Though, your bodyguard and the son of Duke Nightfellow are prepared for such an eventuality."

H-he's got a point!

Derek and Klifford were both dressed for battle—they could fight at a moment's notice. They were even already in their battle stances! Unlike a certain princess I could mention, whose brain was preoccupied with the secret passageway.

But wait a minute...

"For somebody so perceptive of the danger, you're acting awfully natural."

"As I'm unarmed, my only choice is to flee anyway. I shall leave the fighting to those two gentlemen," Rust drawled, casually waving a hand at them.

And as all of this happened, there was no sign of anybody running up the stairs to check on the noise.

"It would seem...that even our intruder friends met with some unforeseen circumstances."

It's almost like they don't have the forces to spare on us... Which means we've got a tailwind, baby! We must ride this wave of good fortune all the way through the passageway.

Just as I was about to declare "*Make haste to Lord Sil!—*"

"Unforeseen... Like, how the son of Duke Nightfellow was here?" Rust asked, turning to Derek accusingly.

"What are you trying to say?" came Derek's icy answer.

"Why did you come to the Sky Chamber in search of Burks? Of course, your judgment was correct. But that was only possible for a limited number of people. There are just two plausible explanations. One, you had a hunch—or some privileged information like me. Or two..."

"*...Derek was in league with the traitors.*" ...is what he likely refrained from saying.

"Are you going to just conveniently forget that it was I who toppled those fake guards?"

"Perhaps *that* was the unforeseen circumstances that befell the intruders? If you wish to deny my claims, then I'd love to hear an explanation of why you thought to come here to look for Burks."

Rust's words rang true. Why *did* Derek come to the Sky Chamber in the first place? That mystery remained unanswered.

"Your Highness, I am quite happy to guide you beyond this point. However, I would like to avoid traveling in the company of someone who might stab me in the back. Do you not have any misgivings about the son of Duke Nightfellow?"

"No…I do not."

Except, like, a little while ago.

"Well, well, well."

"Friend or foe, if I had to choose, I would say that Derek is a friend of Sil. So it's much more likely that he had a hunch, not that he's in league with the traitors."

Since he was surprised to hear that an Adjutant was after Sil, he must have speculated differently than Rust… It might have even been from a source that he's not at liberty to name.

Derek sighed deeply. "Princess Octavia, allow me to explain." He then turned to face me. "House Nightfellow has deep ties with the royal family. As such, we gather all sorts of intelligence—regardless of authenticity. At times, we gather more intelligence than even the royal family itself. While my level of clearance is not as high as my father's, I am privy to a lot of this intelligence…

"I learned that there was something hidden in the Sky Chamber long ago. And when I studied the blueprints of Paradise in the Sky, I noticed several abnormal points in the layout… Be that as it may, actually searching the Sky Chamber was not physically possible for me."

"And that alone was enough to connect Burks to the Sky Chamber? My, what a keen sense of perception you have, son of Duke Nightfellow."

"I made the connection—by my father's behavior regarding the Sky Chamber." Derek curtly nipped Rust's sarcasm in the bud.

"Your…father?" I blurted out under my breath.

Uncle Dearest? Really?

Derek looked at my stunned face and faltered a little before continuing. "I had predicted that my father would set some sort of trap at the junior ball today. Our house did send quite a few men here. Then, when

Countess Reddington gave me permission to carry a weapon, that gave me the opportunity to learn of the venue's security situation...and it was far more heavily guarded than an ordinary junior ball. The extra deployment was probably my father's idea. However, two oddities gave me pause. First, that the garden's security was abnormally light. It was almost begging to be invaded."

"Well, that's because..."

"Yes, as I explained earlier, Princess Octavia, that was a trap my father set to catch the anti-royalist intruders. I figured as much, so I didn't perceive the weak garden security to be much of a problem. What bothered me the most was the second oddity."

"The second oddity?" I filled the brief pause in his speech.

"The guards at the Sky Chamber... Their numbers were not increased. My father would *never* make such a mistake." Derek's tone was firm. "Normally, he would increase the guards' numbers in that area—especially since, as the head of House Nightfellow, he knows of the Sky Chamber's secrets. Regardless, I can only conclude that this action was deliberate. Now...if the junior ball had ended uneventfully, I could have set these thoughts aside as needless worries."

But then Sil disappeared...

"When I learned that Sil was missing, the reason why I headed directly here was because, compared to the main hall, the security here was cleverly weakened. In fact"—Derek paused, casting a bitter glance at the two fake guards lying on the ground—"my father could have quelled this disturbance if he wanted to. And yet the Sky Chamber was left in a state where it was easy to trespass—and it could only have been done on *purpose*."

"An impressive deduction," Rust said in awe.

"Uncle Dearest..." *What were you thinking?* My mind was so blank I even forgot to call him Duke.

"Please, don't misinterpret my words—as far as I can tell, my father is not your enemy, Princess Octavia. Even if he behaves suspiciously, he would never put you in harm's way. But I cannot guarantee that he would show the same grace to anyone else. And besides...the gap in security was my misjudgment, through and through. My father surely had his reasons."

"Yes… I suppose you're right." I nodded.

Yeah. I get it. If I want to know what Uncle Dearest was thinking, I just have to ask him myself. Once we find Lord Sil and bring him back to safety, I'll go speak with Uncle Dearest!

Derek addressed Rust. "So. Does this clear your suspicions of me?"

"Yes, I suppose I can trust the son of Duke Nightfellow to stand at my back. May I offer my humble apologies… Now, Princess Octavia. May the son of Duke Nightfellow accompany us to find Burks?" he asked, getting my permission for good measure.

"What do you say, Lord Derek?"

"We share the same goal. Though if I may be frank, Princess, I don't think you should go—" Derek cast a glance at Rust and sighed. Having the Sky Chamber as a clear target was nice while it lasted, but from this point on, he would have no choice but to adapt to whatever was thrown at him.

He was forced to rely upon Rust, against his will. And the only reason Rust was helping us find Sil was because I had agreed to his provision of accompanying him. Derek seemed to have gotten wind of the negotiations that had brought us to this point. But his suspicion of Rust was just as strong as it was from the very start.

"As a vassal to Esfia's royal family, it is my sworn duty to accompany you," Derek said, pulling the vassal card. "I humbly offer my services."

38

We were in the secret passageway revealed by a mechanism on the throne. From its entrance, there were stairs—at a rather gentle slope—that split into three different directions. Each path was broad with high ceilings. It was not the narrow kind of staircase where you had to walk in single file.

The underground passageway... From our current location, I suppose it was more like a tunnel carved into the mountain behind Paradise in the Sky. Like an artificial mole tunnel.

Was it built with large groups in mind? Maybe it was originally created for military purposes.

Stones that illuminated the darkness were affixed to the passage's walls. The white stone of the wall glowed faintly, helping us see. The secret passageway in the royal castle had the same configuration. You could walk through it just fine without a lantern or a torch. And while it was still dark, it was light enough that you could see your companion's facial expressions when they were close, and there were no hindrances in your walking.

Hmmm, either way, there's something about this...? I inhaled deeply as I walked. *Yup... The air isn't that dusty or moldy.*

I had walked through the secret passageway in the royal castle, too. The sections that were still in service were fine, but when we stepped into the abandoned areas, boy, was I at my wit's end. Now, I was a trooper about it because I had Alec with me, of course! But just by moving slightly, piles of dust flew up into the air and threw us both into an eternal coughing fit.

This passageway, on the other hand... Considering it had been abandoned since King Eus's reign, it was clean—*too* clean. Too clean to be Rust's passageway that led to Sil.

Did somebody clean this passageway so the traitors would have an easier time kidnapping Sil? I don't think so—I can tell from walking in it now that it wasn't one of those things where they did a quick clean of an area that's been closed off for years.

And now that I think about it, the mechanism that opened up this passageway is hundreds of years old, yet it still worked today without a hitch. That's—weird. It's almost like everything was cared for all this time. Like they were expecting visitors today.

Even though this passageway only went one direction—

The mechanism on the throne had a little quirk. From the Sky Chamber side, you could open or close the passageway entrance at will. Both were possible. But from the passageway side, all you could do was close it. The secret passageway in the royal castle had a similar trap in its door—a trap that I fell for epically. Nothing beat the sense of doom that fell over me when I found that the door I'd just opened was shut tight for some reason.

But according to Rust, the entrance in the Sky Chamber wasn't the only one. What's more, the mechanism in the Sky Chamber was the most reliable to operate. So if there was another entrance, I'm sure you'd need a map to be able to navigate it without getting lost.

So what about Sil...? How did he get inside this secret passageway? I stared at Rust's back as he walked ahead of us. *Even if I accept the premise that Rust is indeed going to take us to Sil, I must also assume he has some sort of purpose behind his actions, right? Yeah, duh.*

I gathered my wits about me and lengthened my stride. Thanks to my comfortable dress and low-heeled shoes, it was easy for me to walk—even at a quick pace. I was following directly behind Rust. Klifford walked on my right-hand side, Derek on my left. Since I was our weakest link, they'd positioned themselves protectively on either side of me. We'd reasoned it was much more likely that danger would come from ahead of us rather than from behind.

As we walked along the secret passage, the only sound we heard was that of our own footsteps. It didn't feel like some bad guy would, like, suddenly jump out at us. The air was cold and quiet. However, in atmospheres like this, my senses were not too reliable.

Okay, Klifford... Gimme a reading on the situation! I stole a glance at Klifford. And...he looked neutral. His hand was not at his sword. If he had sensed the presence of another human being—like the Adjutant—he would spring into action. So that meant we weren't in any immediate danger.

That being said, shouldn't he maybe give us some instructions? Then again, though we may seem safe now, there are other enemies we haven't met yet. And talking would break our concentration and make noise, so I guess that's out...

"Is something the matter, Your Highness?" Klifford asked, turning to look at me in the dim light. His eyes met mine.

Did he notice? That I was focusing on him...? I decided to be direct. "Would it be a problem if I spoke with you right now? The traitors might jump out at any minute."

"It wouldn't be a problem. What do you wish to speak with me about?"

"I just wanted to ask... What can I do to make it easier for you to fight? I can't fight myself, you see."

Awaiting battle orders, sir! When the fighting broke out, I was sure to get in the way, so I needed instructions. Like, *"Run like hell into that corner over there!"* If I knew in advance what I should do, I think I'd kinda feel less like dead weight!

"Just act as you normally would while under my guard, Your Highness. Do as you please."

Klifford's calm answer betrayed my fighting spirit's expectations.

"I should...do as I please?"

"Yes."

I'm...not sure how I feel about that. "But what if I were to charge at the traitors? Wouldn't that bother you?" *Not like I'd even do something so scary!*

"I would topple them before you could reach them. You needn't mind me, Your Highness. I shall fight according to your needs. So you may do as you please. Naturally, if you wish to instruct my actions, you may."

Aha... The wheels in my head turned. *I think I get it now. He probably isn't saying I should, like, act recklessly or anything...*

"So you're saying I should make good use of you, yes?"

A small, smile-like shape formed on Klifford's lips.

Okay, well, glad that's cleared up... But is the plan really just Lean on Klifford? Just as I was pondering this, a voice spoke ahead of me.

"What a paragon of grit your bodyguard is—credit where credit is due. To think that he would remain calm and poised when his opponent might be an *Adjutant*..."

Rust continued to talk without looking back at us. "Skilled though our royal bodyguard may be, how do you think we shall deal with this Adjutant if it comes to a sword fight, son of Duke Nightfellow?"

"Will my thinking about it affect the outcome at all?" Derek retorted with another question.

"Fair point—no amount of planning in advance would change the fact that the one after Burks is an *Adjutant*," Rust concluded with a chuckle in his voice.

Then Derek, who'd had a thoughtful fist pressed to his chin, looked at me and said gravely, "Is it true? Is there really an Adjutant involved in this conspiracy?"

Back in the Sky Chamber, when Rust had thrown in the word *Adjutant*, Derek had gasped and looked gravely concerned. But that conversation had been left sort of unresolved, as you may recall.

"According to Rust, yes. Though whether you believe him or not is your choice, Lord Derek."

"Princess Octavia... Do *you* believe an Adjutant is involved?"

The symbol on Sil's guardian ring popped into my mind. Because of that image, I couldn't just laugh it off and tell Derek he was out of his mind.

Derek pressed me further. "*That guy's* claims aside, do you have any reason to believe an Adjutant is involved with this conspiracy?"

That made me curious. *He's asking whether an Adjutant is after Sil... and not if Adjutants even exist in the first place? Has Derek believed in them all along?*

"Lord Derek—do you have any knowledge regarding Adjutants?"

"The Saza Church's..." But Derek thought better of it and shut his mouth. "Never mind."

The Saza Church? The Saza Church and Adjutants? It's no use... I couldn't find any recollection of either of those two terms from *The Noble King* lore in my past-life memory, and nothing that I'd experienced or learned in my present life as Octavia was helping me make any connections, either.

"If I learn anything definite, I will tell you," he promised.

Though I was dying with curiosity, the only proper response to that was to nod in understanding.

Adjutants... Thinking about it, it's pretty strange that Adjutants have a connection with the Sky Chamber. When the secret passageway opened up in the Sky Chamber, I was like, "But how?"

"How did the Adjutant...?" My curiosity spilled out of me in a murmur.

"How?" Rust repeated back to me.

"The mechanism on the throne that opens this secret passageway... How did the Adjutant who's after Lord Sil know about all of this?"

My father—the king—might have known about this secret passageway. And so did Duke Nightfellow—Uncle Dearest. That much is clear. I wouldn't be surprised if either of them knew about it.

Alec's face popped into my mind, but I shook it off and refocused on my train of thought.

But what about the Adjutant? He's not the king, and he's not the duke, who's had a long-standing intimate relationship with the royal family. This isn't the sort of intel that's easily come by. So does this have something to do with the fact that somebody's been doing routine maintenance on this passageway?

"Could it be because an Adjutant served King Eus?" Rust submitted a long-standing theory. "I've heard that Adjutants have a strong sense of camaraderie. What if this information was shared among them and passed down through the generations?"

"Is that possible, though?" I asked. "There's no proof that King Eus valued his Adjutant. King Eus's regard of Adjutants may very well have been the opposite."

As a devout *fujoshi* who surrendered to her fangirlish desires and devoured all the written works of King Eus's life, I could not possibly have any blind spots—well, I guess I could—but I still could not endorse Rust's theory.

If an Adjutant served King Eus, then that would have to mean that Eus was a Sovereign. And I don't think he'd make such a pact. King Eus was revered as the restorer of the Esfian dynasty. However, there were two times in history—his ascension to the throne and after it—where public opinion of King Eus was contradictory. He was mostly revered during his governance immediately after his enthronement.

At the beginning of his reign, he had a vassal and an Adjutant, both of whom he relied upon heavily. That was the favored version of the story. Adjutants serving certain kings and heroes of legend were usually added into the stories for dramatic effect.

And this practice wasn't exclusive to Esfia.

With a little help from Cissy—my bookworm friend and translator—I was able to read old epics from our neighboring kingdom of Khangena. Those books also had nameless Adjutants coloring their pages.

But shortly after his enthronement, King Eus determined that Adjutants' battle prowess was a threat. He avoided Adjutants altogether ever since. This information appears not only in the storybooks, but in many official records as well. So it's highly credible.

So. Back to the two diametrically opposed views on King Eus. It's said that public opinion of King Eus changed because, once crowned, he'd grown into a very different person. But a thought hit me—if everything King Eus accomplished was done by just one person...then the story didn't add up.

But what if King Eus was actually two people? What if the king everyone hated and the king everyone revered had been shoehorned into one person? And who was this other person, you might ask? I had a certain character in mind—King Eus's elder sister, the former queen.

If it was true that the crown had an Adjutant in its employ at the beginning of King Eus's reign, that probably actually happened when the queen was in power. If you hypothesize that the Adjutant actually served the queen, then it all made sense.

"It seems, Your Highness, that you are suggesting that while King

Eus did heavily rely upon an Adjutant at the start of his reign, a certain incident caused him to despise Adjutants."

Rust's words snapped me out of my thoughts. "A certain incident?"

"The drastic change in King Eus occurred after the rebellion against him led by the head of House Alderton, correct? Ah yes, come of think of it, your bodyguard hails from House Alderton, doesn't he? What an *interesting* coincidence."

Count Alderton led a rebellion against King Eus right after he was enthroned. He was painted as a villain from the very start in *The Legend of King Eus*. That's right… That was *the* Count Alderton!

The rebellion itself was written in bullet points from start to finish. Oddly enough, it was what happened *after* it—the worship and adoration of King Eus, who let the mastermind who schemed the usurpation off the hook with a light punishment—that was spelled out in great detail!

"Though it has closely served the royal family, House Alderton has been shunned due to its misdeeds in the past. Why did you select someone from that house to be your bodyguard, Your Highness?"

Because memories of my past life compelled me to do eeny-meeny-miny-moe… It was Japan! Through and through. I was sorta asking Japan's deities for guidance. Alderton… Aside from the fact that they're a house of counts known for their military prowess and that they only give birth to girls, I had nothing about them in my memory! Though, if I'd given it a little thought after I'd heard Klifford's name for the first time, I would have remembered…maybe.

Was that why Alec acted weird when he heard Klifford's name? No, wait, it's not like Klifford or the present-day Count Alderton did anything wrong!

"Is that even a question worth asking?" I retorted. "Are you suggesting that, after all these centuries, Count Alderton is plotting to harm the crown again?"

"Lower-class noblemen like myself aside, aren't most people surprised to see him in your service? Especially people…who come from that great noble family who's been around since ancient times."

That great noble family who's been around since ancient times...

"What do *you* think, Lord Derek?"

Derek smirked. "Me? I think nothing of it. Your bodyguard hailing from House Alderton is of little consequence—it's strange to equate the past with the present."

My relief in having someone agree with me was fleeting. A new misgiving popped into my mind.

"I wonder if Sirius disagrees with you?" I asked.

During the opening dance with Derek, I'd gleaned the information that my big brother had a bad impression of Klifford. Maybe it was fueled by a negative bias against House Alderton altogether.

"He has the same opinion I do," Derek assured me. "Sirius doesn't see Alderton's lineage itself as problematic."

Alderton's lineage..."itself"? Aren't we kinda beating around the bush here, Derek?

We made our way down the passageway as we talked. And just when we were turning left at a fork in the stairs, it happened.

Klifford was the first to react.

In the passageway ahead of us...several men were lying on the ground.

They weren't dead. They weren't bleeding.

There were six of them—all men—and they were dressed for battle.

Sil was not among them. If anything, these were the men who were after him...I think. They were ambushed by someone—or something—and tried to fight back but were toppled in a flash. That's the impression I got from the sight of them.

"They weren't killed... That's unfathomable," Derek murmured after he finished inspecting the intruders with just as much finesse as Klifford. It was a bit surprising to see this level of skill from the son of a duke, but he'd been just as perceptive back in the Sky Chamber, when he had the wisdom to take the weapons away from the unconscious fake soldiers so they would be rendered incapable of fighting.

Since we had nothing with which to tie them up, Derek and Klifford used their teeth to tear pieces of their uniforms into strips and bound their wrists with that. The former looked awfully familiar with the process.

Rust had said, "There's no guarantee I won't act suspiciously. Letting those two gentlemen handle the task would surely put you at ease, Your Highness." —Basically, he used the same tactic this time that he'd used with the fake guards earlier to get out of doing the work.

"Do you suppose their assailants were overwhelmingly powerful?" I suggested.

Derek shook his head. "Perhaps so, but their assailants would have been wise to silence them for good—to make sure no vital information was leaked. Unless they wanted to question them, their assailants gained no advantage by keeping them alive," Derek declared, in a way that suggested that's what he would have done.

"But what if their assailants were friendly with them? That might make them hesitate to take their lives." *Or here's another theory:* "What about the possibility that Lord Sil was the one who toppled them?"

"That would be a valid explanation as to why they're still alive...but that would mean that Sil is such an overwhelming force that he could overpower many opponents at once without spilling a drop of blood."

From the way Derek spoke, it sounded like Sil's Solo Flawless Victory was kinda maybe impossible. Too bad; I thought it was definitely a possibility... I mean, I read the books...

"Did something pique your interest, Klifford?" I asked as he rose from his kneeling position beside one of the fallen intruders. He was holding the man's longsword. He slid it out smoothly from its sheath. Its blade gleamed—it was engraved with lined markings.

"All six of them were carrying Turchen swords. They've been well used, and I can tell from their physiques that these men were quite capable. And yet they were all put out of commission in such a small area before they could flee. I believe their assailant might have been an Adjutant."

"An Adjutant... But I heard that Adjutants weren't as forgiving as their assailant clearly was." Derek looked down at the six men who were merely unconscious.

Klifford returned the Turchen sword to its red sheath. "Well...this Adjutant may have been benevolent." When Klifford said this, there was a look of scorn on his face.

39

Maybe he left them alive for questioning... Otherwise, does such an Adjutant exist? An Adjutant who would leave his opponents alive at the cost of his own advantage without a good reason for doing so? I'm not sure why, but I had a feeling Klifford knew of such an Adjutant.

Adjutants had a strong sense of camaraderie. There were many a tale about this in the tomes of Khangenan mythology I'd read. It's just, even if such an Adjutant did exist, in my headcanon, Klifford was a lone-wolf sort of Adjutant... But it just felt more *right* to me to think that Klifford *had* met another Adjutant besides himself, even if the opposite was really the case.

Wait... As Klifford's Sovereign, aren't I the only one who knows he's an Adjutant? Among living human beings, that is... So wouldn't it be weird if he knew any other Adjutants? Oh, or maybe he's heard whispers about other Adjutants, or he's acquainted with other Adjutants, but they don't know he's an Adjutant. Like, that sort of deal?

After that train of thought was exhausted, I looked up into those indigo eyes. I was going to finally just go ahead and ask him—but I regained my senses.

No, Octavia. Bad. It's a secret that he's an Adjutant and I'm his Sovereign. I can't ask any questions that might make Derek or Rust catch on to that fact.

Though I was kinda dying to know who the heck knocked out six whole intruders without killing them...

"However, if that's the case..." Derek turned his attention away from the intruders and back to Rust. "Maybe there's more than one Adjutant? A different Adjutant—one who's *not* after Sil? Or maybe they really *are* one and the same?"

Rust shrugged. "I believe their assailant being an Adjutant was the bodyguard's hypothesis—though rather than ask me, wouldn't it be best to just ask the ones who were there? Their assailant's soft heart was their salvation. They are only unconscious. We could shake them awake and get our answer from them directly."

Derek shook his head at that idea. "Their mouths won't open so easily... And we don't have enough time to give them a thorough interrogation. We would need a few days, at least."

"How can you be so sure?" Rust asked.

Derek touched the left side of his neck. "They all have a tattoo right here. Everyone who has this tattoo has one thing in common: Rather than be tortured until they spit out their secrets out of sheer desperation, they will try to kill themselves. That's what they're like."

Tattoos on their necks? I strained my eyes and looked at the area in question. *Whoa, yeah... Tattoos, all right.* It was then that a sudden question crossed my mind: *Insignias? Maybe the tattoos resemble Insignias?* But I was wrong. *I wonder what they are, then? They're some sort of geometric pattern... Oh, I know! One of the sub-characters who showed up just before the Turchen Arc had something just like this...* It was used on the cover design, and it looked so cool that I guess I remembered it.

Let's see... This geometric pattern is... "The crest of the Saza Church, I presume?"

Rust's gaze shot from Derek to me like he was locking onto a new target. He had a suuuper suspicious look in his eyes. I...I *think* it's the Saza Church. Was I wrong?

"Correct—Your Highness," Derek answered. "Saza's elite soldiers of faith are branded with these tattoos as proof of their classification. Since they're trained hard and willing to die, they're difficult adversaries to deal with. I'm just…surprised that you would recognize their crest, Princess. It's different from the crest the Saza Church formally uses."

The subtext—*Where the hell did you learn about that crest?*—was painfully clear.

"Why, I learned it from a BL novel called The Noble King!"

Oh, how easy everything would be if I could just say that.

Let's see, what's a good excuse I can use…? I get the feeling if I give him the wrong answer, this might all blow up in my face. But let's not forget body language, either. It's not like he took me by the shoulders and asked me a serious question. I'll just pretend I didn't notice Derek thinks I'm sus and keep talking.

"You're absolutely right, Lord Derek—it is quite difficult to get the Saza Church's elite soldiers of faith to talk. And we wouldn't want them to commit suicide now, would we? Klifford."

"Yes?"

"Take their weapons and bind them so they cannot escape when they wake."

Many mysteries still remained—Did an Adjutant knock out these intruders? What exactly happened?—but if we can't get these six men to talk right away, then we should render them harmless and proceed onward! Finding Sil comes first.

"Aye." And Klifford went to work.

After staring at me for a while, Derek sighed. "Allow me to help…" And assisted Klifford. And as I stood there, just watching them, my working-class heart cried a little. I really wanted to lend a hand, but as a princess, it was more proper for me to stand idly by and look important. I knew this, and yet…

Another part of me was impatient and anxious, distracting myself by opening and closing Blackfeather. Derek lifted up a sword of one of the unconscious soldiers—it was about as large as it needed to be, considering they were dressed for combat. He hurled it into the distance.

After that, the two men added daggers and other various weapons to the pile.

Maybe I should borrow one of the weapons from the pile? But I quickly revised my idea. *No, if anybody should take a weapon, it's—*

"We've finished tying them up, Your Highness," Klifford announced. They'd accomplished the task with surprising efficiency.

"Thank you."

"Now that we've rendered the elite soldiers of faith harmless, shall we hurry on over to Burks?" Rust suggested, stepping forward to take the lead again.

"Not yet," I said, signaling him to stop. I ran over to the opposite side of where the six men were tied up—rather, to the area where Derek had started the little weapon pile with that first sword he threw.

None of them were adorned with gaudy embellishments. Even my normie eyes could tell these weapons were not for ornamental or ceremonial use—they were weapons for real battle. There was everything from longswords to daggers...to throwing thingies of unsavory purpose.

Then again, recognizing real weapons was one thing. Knowing whether they were any good—I had no frickin' clue. And since I didn't have much time to give it a good long pondering, I went with the safe choice: the longsword... *Yeah, let's go with the one Klifford drew earlier. The sword in the red sheath. He did say it was Turchen-made. I think this's the one?*

I spotted the longsword in question and reached out to it. I grabbed its hilt with both hands—along with my closed fan.

Gee. If only this were light and easy for me to fight with...

"Princess Octavia?"

I heard Derek's voice. I looked up and saw that not only Derek, but Klifford and Rust as well, were all staring at me.

"Your Highness, do you anticipate that you, too, shall cross swords with our Adjutant?" Rust asked in a tone that was both playful and cruel.

"Of course not," I said, approaching Rust, who stood a dozen or so paces away from me. Then I thrust the longsword right in front of his face. "Rust Byrne...it is *you* who will use this sword."

"Me...? But, Your Highness, surely you haven't forgotten my behavior back in the garden?"

"You had no intentions of hurting me, correct? I cannot fight. But, Rust, all you need is a weapon, and you are more than capable of fighting." I stressed the *more than capable* part. That's where Rust and I were very different.

Rust fell silent. He wasn't smiling anymore.

I mean, if this Rust is like he was in the source material, he's totally strong! Strong enough to hold his own in a fight with Sirius. And even if I'm wrong, at the very least, he's a hell of a lot better than I am. It's unfair to deprive the world of your gift, Rust!

And if the worst happens... If the worst happens, and Rust turns his sword on me, I know Klifford will protect me. I've got Derek in my corner, too. So I deemed it would be no problem to give him a sword!

Now, I know this totally wouldn't happen in the first place, but if it were just Rust and me alone in this passageway, whether I would have given him a weapon *then*... Well, that's a touchy subject.

"It is not my wish for you to be toppled by the enemy. Besides, if we add you to our arsenal, that will not only make fighting easier for Klifford and Lord Derek—it will give you a means of protecting yourself as well. I don't think that mask of yours is an effective weapon against anyone other than myself, no?"

Rust was putting himself in just as much danger as I was. And if he stayed unarmed, worst-case scenario, he might leave this story's cast of characters. Unless there was some sort of plot twist like when we get to Sil we find out that Rust was actually in league with the traitors. Either scenario was dangerous—but I decided to put my faith in the former. So I'll give him a longsword to lower his chances of exiting stage left!

"You wanted a weapon, did you not?"

"Yes..." The smile returned to Rust's lips—a neat little arc. "I graciously accept it, and I thank you for your kindness, Princess Octavia."

Rust touched the sword at last, easily lifting it with one hand as if it weighed no more than a single sheet of paper. He studied it. He removed the blade slightly from the sheath, then promptly returned it.

"You gave me the Turchen longsword, I see."

"Does that displease you?"

"Oh, don't be silly. I shall reward your kindness by making my mind as sharp as this sword."

Then he truly took the lead.

It's so terribly—quiet.

The farther down we walked, the spacious—albeit boorish—vibe of the passageway noticeably changed. In a word, it got *luxe*. The white walls with their special glowing stones were replaced with ornate decorations. Sculpted pillars lined our path. If somebody blindfolded me and took me here, I'd have mistaken it for the royal castle at night.

It wasn't a secret passageway anymore—by outward appearances, it was a formal corridor. It was built in such a way that it was hard for me not to imagine royalty and the nobility walking down it.

When we turned a corner, the space suddenly grew bright. I shaded my eyes with my hand and blinked until my eyes adjusted. Lying ahead of us was a perfectly straight corridor. Both sides of the wall were lined with torches, ablaze with fire. Judging by their height, not much time had passed since they were lit.

At the end of the corridor stood one door. It gave me a strange sense of déjà vu...

"The Sky Chamber..."

It was a blue double door. A door I'd opened just once before at Paradise in the Sky.

"Burks is in the *Sky Chamber*...," Rust slowly whispered pointedly to me.

We'd been to the Sky Chamber… But he'd meant *this* Sky Chamber.

"You're missing a word… I think you meant the *other* Sky Chamber."

"Technically, I suppose you're right." Rust chuckled deep in his throat. "If I was to amend my former statement, it would go something like this: Burks is in a place that King Eus loved so deeply that he hid it from the world—he's in the *other* Sky Chamber."

An image of Alec's face materialized in my memory.

"Dear Sister, please don't go in the Sky Chamber."

And it made me think…that maybe when my beloved little brother begged me not to go in the Sky Chamber, it was *this* Sky Chamber. One that you might call the *true* Sky Chamber.

40

The first thing I saw was—blue.

The natural walls, coloring the whole room. Clear blue crystals shone on each of the four walls. On the ceiling, too. An artist had painted the portions of the ceiling to depict the sky in its morning, noon, and nighttime states.

It was a perfect marriage of natural and artificial—this room of blue. Its beauty was captivating.

The Sky Chamber—this was the room to which that name referred. The room in Paradise in the Sky that had come to be known as the Sky Chamber was actually a replica of this room.

We were in the throne room in King Eus's villa—and the walls echoed with the clanging sound of swords.

The moment we opened the double doors, an intruder lunged at us. Klifford jumped in front and countered. Derek and Rust swung their swords soon after. All the enemies at the door fell back in a wave.

But a quick glance showed that a dozen or so enemies still

remained in the Sky Chamber. Most of them were wearing hooded cloaks that obscured their faces. They were all looking at us, swords brandished high.

I quickly gripped Blackfeather by its hilt and snapped it closed. For a moment, the clanging swords quieted. The traitors were frozen still.

I took a deep breath. *I am woman, hear me roar. If I'm gonna carry out the plan I suggested before we came in here, it's now or never.*

I promptly opened Blackfeather and began a sonorous address. "Good evening, esteemed intruders." My Princess Smile shone, clashing hard with the mood in the room. "And also—I believe there's an Adjutant with you?" I pressed Blackfeather to my lips, feigning an air of casual confidence. "Would you like to have a little chat with Esfia's princess?"

I'd made my move. Now the question was: How would they react? Each passing second dragged on longer than the last. I shifted Blackfeather slightly upward.

"The princess of Esfia… Are you the real thing?" one of the hooded men murmured. There was a hoarseness in his voice. He could be rather old. The other intruders shot questioning looks at him.

So this guy's their leader? I continued, finally finding my in. "Are you suggesting I am a fake? Well, there may be two Sky Chambers, but there is only one princess of Esfia, and she is I."

Silence fell. It felt like we were at an impasse. Then Klifford—sensing something—moved a little from his place in front of me.

"Stand down." The leader commanded at the same time—but not to us. Just as his voice sounded, the man beside him froze. The rest of the intruders obeyed the man's command and showed no further sign of coming closer to us.

"Princess Octavia," the man said, addressing me personally this time. His face was hidden, but I could clearly see his jet-black eyes staring into mine. "I do not recall inviting you to join us here."

"For that, I apologize. In my search for someone, I found myself here."

"Searching for someone?"

"Yes—a man by the name of Sil Burks."

I—I still sound confident AF, though, right? Keep it together, Octavia! Don't let them hear your silent screams of terror over this touch-and-go situation!

I was trying to soften the mood a little before the room erupted into an all-out war. I was using my position as princess to open negotiations.

I am a princess—in other words, I'm the shit! It doesn't matter how wimpy I am on the inside. My power as princess trumps that. That's why it really meant something that I was extending a diplomatic hand. High-status individuals always make the best diplomats—the other side is much more likely to listen, of course!

From reading *The Legend of King Eus* and all those Khangenan tomes, there was a fact of which I became acutely aware: Prebattle negotiations were beyond crucial. And while my current situation was much smaller in scale, it was still the same.

Even though I'd read those books as a rabid fujoshi—no, *because* I'd read those books as a rabid fujoshi, I remembered every detail! If the negotiations went well, then great. The dispute was resolved peacefully, and there was much rejoicing. And if the negotiations failed... Well, they still seldom made the situation any worse than it already was. The war just went ahead as scheduled. If anything, opening negotiations gave you a window to assess the enemy's position.

Now's the time to lead with diplomacy! I was worried the enemy wouldn't respond to me, but we've cleared that hurdle!

"It surprises me that a princess would trouble herself searching for just one man... What is your purpose?"

"Lord Sil is the lover of my brother—Crown Prince Sirius. He's very dear to us. Isn't that enough reason for me to search for him?" As I talked, I scanned the Sky Chamber for any sign of Sil... But he wasn't immediately visible.

Is he not in here? No... He has to be here.

I sharpened my senses and looked around the room again. And the navy-blue hair I'd missed earlier caught my eye this time. That hair belonged to Sil.

Found him!

He was in the deepest nook of the Sky Chamber, hunched over something that served as a sort of platform. *Is he unconscious? Is he wounded?*

My eyes scanned the ground beneath him, searching for anything that resembled a pool of blood... And I sighed in relief. *No blood...I think. But I can't get a better idea of how Sil's doing without getting closer...*

Just as I thought this, Klifford took a step forward—from my diagonal to directly in front of me.

"I thought I told you to stand down...," the leader said, hindering the hooded figure's sword again. "Did your *Sovereign* command you to take that action as well?"

From the look of things, this was the same soldier the man had commanded to stand down earlier. Only the would-be attacker's eyes were visible from beneath the hood—eyes as clear blue as the crystals that decorated the Sky Chamber.

And from the words *your Sovereign's command*, it was clear—this was our Adjutant.

But wait... This guy had been locking swords with our jet-black-eyed leader friend when we first entered the Sky Chamber. There were nineteen intruders total in here. Two were toppled immediately after we entered. And Klifford, Derek, and Rust subdued the three who had charged at us.

Meaning, the reason not many men attacked us when we entered was because there was already a battle taking place inside the Sky Chamber—and the two men on the ground had been defeated by this guy. At least, that's my theory. And maybe this guy was the Adjutant who'd spared the lives of those elite soldiers of faith?

If he's against the intruders, then maybe we can form an alliance? No, wait, he tried to attack me before the leader stopped him. Twice, at that. That's why Klifford wanted to attack him.

*And the guy who stopped him from attacking me was the intruders'
leader...who's after Sil and is also our enemy...*

My brain started to hurt.

"It wasn't my Sovereign's command...," the Adjutant answered—he
had the voice of a young man.

"I'm not surprised."

"But Esfia's royal family is merely—"

As I watched the Adjutant and the black-eyed man argue out of the
corner of my eye, Derek stepped backward to my side and whispered,
"We have an ally among them."

By "them," he means the intruders, right? We have an...ally?

"The slender man with red hair." Derek said no more and stepped
away from me again.

Slender... Red hair... I followed Derek's line of vision at first, but the
man turned out to be in the opposite direction. He wasn't wearing a
hood—he was dressed in formal attire. He'd probably slipped in with
the first party here. He was in his late twenties, and his face wasn't
familiar to me. However...

*Oh! That physique, that hair, that outfit. If you put a mask on him...
wouldn't he look just like the guy who asked Klifford to dance back at
the pleasaunce hall?* He was also my second dance partner in the Hof-
balltanze. The deceptively suave player.

*Since Derek vouched for him, does that mean he's with House Night-
fellow? Like, as one of Uncle Dearest's subordinates?*

"I can't say I don't sympathize with you. But at least stay put until
we're finished talking," the man told the Adjutant, lowering his sword.
The Adjutant lowered his sword obligingly—albeit reluctantly.

I turned my focus back to them.

"Now then—my apologies, Princess. So what is it you wish from
us?" The man turned to look pointedly back into the deep recesses of
the Sky Chamber—he knew I'd spotted Sil.

"My *wish* is that you gentlemen release Lord Sil and surrender."

"Surrender? Us?" The man sounded as though he was about to

laugh. "It is *you* who should leave this place. *I* have no interest in the royal family. As long as you stay out of my way, I'll have no reason to kill you."

"What do you want…? Is Lord Sil your only target?"

"That's right."

"Why Lord Sil, pray tell? And what did you do to him?"

"He's still alive…" His response was vague. But it confirmed that Sil was indeed merely unconscious.

"Do you mean to say you won't harm him?"

"Princess. You would be wise to go back to where you're supposed to be."

"Maybe *you* should stop and consider the significance behind my being here. Do you honestly think an esteemed princess such as I would storm into an enemy nest with only a handful of men?"

Even though that's kind of exactly what I did!

My bluff was met with silence.

"In a few moments, a large platoon of soldiers will storm the Sky Chamber," I continued. "I don't suppose even an Adjutant would be capable of holding them all off? I'm here as an act of goodwill toward you *gentlemen*. I'm giving you a chance to surrender."

"Nonsense. A princess does not have the authority to dispatch the royal army."

The man has a point!

My eyes almost started darting furtively about. But I somehow managed to keep them glued to the man before me. I could just see the redheaded ally Derek pointed out earlier in my peripheral vision.

Then a thought struck me—it didn't have to be the royal army.

"Who said anything about the royal army? Mobilizing a private army of noble soldiers loyal to me is well within my purview."

The jet-black eyes shot to Derek. "House Nightfellow's private army…"

Yup. Let's go with that.

"Do you understand now?"

"Yes…I understand, Princess." The man nodded silently.

So I guess he kinda believes Uncle Dearest's private army is on the way? Good. Now if he'll just back off…

"I understand…that I must be vigilant," came his disturbing reply. "My Adjutant status made me arrogant—I underestimated you, Princess."

So this man is also an Adjutant… Things just took a dark turn.

"Lend me a hand," the man told the other Adjutant. Seeing the Adjutant nod and join his side, the man continued, "I will not surrender. Neither will I release my prisoner. Though it seems *you* will not surrender, either. So before Nightfellow's private army arrives, I have no choice but to dispose of you, *Princess.*"

The man threw off his robe, signaling there was no longer a need to hide his identity. My gaze locked with his jet-black eyes—reminiscent of a bird of prey. I tried to stare just as menacingly in return.

It was time for combat.

The intruders, with the two Adjutants at their head, charged at me.

"Brace yourself…"

"Fear not, I shall live up to the fine Turchen blade Her Highness gave me, son of Duke Nightfellow."

"I really hope you will."

Derek and Rust assumed defensive stances.

My negotiations…were an epic fail. I felt weak in the knees. But there was a silver lining. Sil was now unguarded.

"Klifford. I'm going to Lord Sil."

"I'll cover you." Klifford moved without a noise, parrying the still-hooded Adjutant's first attack. A tremendous *clang* split my ears.

"*You…?*" the younger Adjutant murmured just as I took off running.

I just have to run to Sil. Don't think about anything else.

There was a golden throne in this Sky Chamber, too.

Go behind it—

Sil was hunched over a platform of some sort. There was an unsheathed sword on the ground right beside him. I touched him.

He's warm. The guy did say he was still alive, but he definitely is breathing. He has a pulse, too. And he's not wounded. He's just unconscious...asleep, more like.

A sigh of relief spilled out of me.

I pulled Sil off the platform and onto the ground...and it was then that I noticed the thing Sil had been hunched over was not an ordinary platform...

It was a cenotaph. Made of the same blue crystals that decorated the Sky Chamber. It was shaped like the cenotaphs used in Esfian royal burials.

The most significant aspect was the name engraved in the crystal. I traced it with my fingertips.

—*Idéalia Esfia*

Esfia's royalty did not take a surname. If I did, I'd be Octavia Esfia. But that was an honor not permitted to other royalty. It was actually more proper for royalty to have no surname.

Only one type of person in the royal family was allowed to use the name of Esfia—the ones who had been crowned. Like the current king, my father: Enoch Esfia.

Throughout history, only kings were allowed to use the surname Esfia...in life and in death. Idéalia was a woman's name. Her surname of Esfia signaled that she once reigned as queen.

"Queen...Idéalia."

When Paradise in the Sky was the royal family's villa, this room must have been used as the throne room.

So...was this Sky Chamber...her tomb?

My father said her very name had been erased from the records.

Is this really the tomb of the queen? The queen...who was killed by her little brother, King Eus?

King Eus hid it, yet he kept it safe.

It was Rust... When I was talking to Rust, in the garden.

I caught movement out of the corner of my eye. I looked toward it with a start. Sil was squirming on the ground. He slowly opened his eyes and got to his feet. Then he silently picked up his fallen sword.

"Lord Sil, how are you feel—?" But I couldn't finish my question.

In a flash, Sil closed the distance between us. Klifford stepped between us, hooked me in his left arm, and jumped backward.

And into the empty space where I had been, a sword slashed.

It was Sil's sword.

41

The second attack came immediately after. Klifford held me with his left arm while blocking the attack with the sword in his right, slashing it away.

Sil stumbled, but only for a moment. He dodged Klifford's counter-attack and struck again. Sil's movements were anything but ordinary. They were smooth, almost like a dance. But most notable of all was the fact that he was holding his own against Klifford. Their swords locked. They fiercely pushed against each other.

"Lord Sil!" I cried.

But he wouldn't answer me. All traces of nuance were gone from Sil's expressive face. He looked like a puppet.

Is this what I think it is…?

"Hey, Maki!"

A conversation from my past life popped into my head. I'd been subconsciously avoiding thinking about my past, because I could never keep my shitty haunting memories from popping up. This included daily life with my family and silly yet precious moments with my friends.

"You know those books you loaned me, Maki? Is there a part three?"

"Oh, cool! Which one are ya talking about? Go ahead and take

whatever you—oh, The Noble King? But that's a Boys Love series! You're a shoujo manga gal, aren't you, Sis? What happened to you?!"

"Well, I *was gonna just borrow some shoujo manga at first, but I noticed you had several copies of the same volumes, and it made me curious."*

"Well, duh, it's The Noble King! *This one is my copy for personal use—I can read it as many times as I like without worrying it'll get messed up. This one is a copy for lending to others when I want to spread the gospel. The one with the protective cover is to keep it in mint condition. Buying multiple copies of the same volume is fujoshi 101 stuff!"*

"Oooh, in that case, rejoice, Maki! *Thy gospel-spreading copy hath produced thy first* Noble King *convert! Boys Love is actually pretty awesome! It's a whole new world. So do you have Volume 3?"*

"Holy shit... *Well, Volume 2 is the latest in the series. Volume 3 doesn't come out until next month."*

"Lame. *So wait, does this mean we have to wait until the next volume to find out how our hero was saved? To find out who defeated all those enemies? I'm not liking the vagueness here!"*

"Um, *obviously Sil awakened to his true powers!"*

"You mean the hero? Lame. Maki, you're wrong—it's gotta be Sirius *or some whole new hero. Sil was just a decoy hero to fool us until the epic plot twist."*

"Dude, it's Sil!"

"No, it's Sirius or a new surprise hero!"

My first successful convert was my big sister in my past life. And Volume 2 was the first time Sil's trance came up. After rereading it, though, I realized there were glimpses of it in Volume 1's illustrations, too.

In one scene, Sil is surrounded by enemies, staring death in the face! But he loses consciousness there. *Blackout.* Then, in the next scene, all the enemies are lying at his feet. The story doesn't explain who defeated

Sil's assailants. What's more, incidents of a similar nature happened in the following volumes many times.

Was it Sirius…or a new character? I kept bouncing back and forth between the two theories. But there was one major clue in the last volume I'd read—one of the illustrations strongly implied it was Sil. Then again…I'm really just going off vibes here. The question still hadn't been resolved in the story proper yet.

"Hey, Sis! Did you read the latest volume?! Man, that fighting scene between Sil and Sirius, right?! The conflict in Sirius was so beautifully tragic!"

"Oh, Maki. So young. So naive. We still know nothing until the next volume comes out. There might be a big plot twist in store."

"Oh, Sis, just let it go already…"

I was Team Sil, and my sister was Team Someone Else. Every time a new volume was released, there were heated discussions between us. Unfortunately…before I could get my hands on the latest volume that supposedly answered that question, I died.

And I might be witnessing it in action right now—among a chain of events that hadn't happened in the source material.

So I was right! It was Sil awakening to his secret powers! Take that, Sis!

His trigger was a mystery. But at times, Sil could unleash astonishing levels of strength. The only catch was: Sil had no memories of this whenever it happened. I just *know* that's the state he's in right now!

"Looks like we have our answer."

Yes! We have our ans—

Somebody had voiced the exact thoughts in my mind with a very odd synchrony. It was the Adjutant who'd just uncovered his face.

Without my noticing, this leader-Adjutant with the jet-black eyes had come very close to me. Like a gust of wind in a straight line. But I wasn't his destination—it was Sil. Had his priorities just changed? Was it now Sil, instead of me, who needed to be disposed of?

And why was it so? Because Sil had become *like that*?

Sil shifted his attention from Klifford to the Adjutant. But before he could counter, the younger Adjutant stood in his way. As if to protect Sil.

Is he on Sil's side?

My brain started to spin. As the duo of Adjutants—who were supposed to be *my* enemy—fought each other, the fight between Klifford and Sil continued.

"Klifford!"

"Wait just a moment, please," Klifford answered. His breathing had remained calm and even all this time. Since he was holding me in one arm as he fought, I could tell just how much leeway he had in this fight. He had so much leeway, in fact, that he was able to hold me so exquisitely that I would remain unharmed.

The fight that looked evenly matched at the start now was clearly Klifford's to win. I'd always thought that Super Sil could hold his own against an Adjutant in a fight—and well, there he was, fighting an Adjutant for real!

But Klifford was able to get the upper hand against Super Sil, even while holding me in one arm. And upon closer glance, the white uniform he'd borrowed had not a drop of blood or schmutz on it.

He's OP... In my past-life lingo, we'd call Klifford an overpowered character, right?

Wait.

Um, it looks like he's about to kinda kill Sil, you knooow?! In a matter of seconds, Sil's on his knees, and Klifford is raising his swooord?! When Klifford said "Wait just a moment, please," did he actually mean "I'll put Sil in an eternal time-out with my sword"? D-did he interpret me calling his name as "Kill him quick, 'kay?" Aaahhh! Yeah, I can see how someone might interpret it that way!

"D-don't kill him, Klifford!" I cried, pounding his left arm around my waist. His arm was abnormally hard. I knew that interfering with his fighting put both our lives at risk, but I couldn't stand idly by and watch.

Klifford gave me a look of protest—a sharp gleam lingered in his indigo eyes. "Burks is attempting to harm you, Your Highness. Is it really necessary to keep him alive?"

I hate being riiight! Yes, it's necessary! Super necessary! Oh, and one more thing! "I don't think he was trying to harm *me*...," I argued, shaking my head.

I thought about it, drawing on my knowledge of the source material. *Let's assume this is Sil's trance state that I'd seen happen many times in the books. That would mean Sil thinks everyone around him is the enemy right now. He just identified me as his enemy because I happened to be closest to him when his Super Sil side awakened. That's why he attacked me. I feel bad using him as an example, but if Derek had been next to Sil when he woke up, I'm sure he'd be in the same predicament as me.*

I mean...in his newest trance rampage in the most recent volume of *The Noble King*, he tried to attack Sirius. He can't be stopped until he believes he's safe—on a primal level. In other words, he won't stop until he, or everyone around him, lies defeated on the ground.

"Sil is not in his right mind at the moment. He's forgotten who he is—"

AGH!

No sooner did I say that than Sil's sword flashed before my eyes.

If Sil's not in his right mind, he won't pause the battle long enough for me to speak! Yup. He definitely will attack me!

Klifford expertly parried the attacks, but since I had been talking, I didn't fare as well. I lost my footing and flung my arms around Klifford's neck to regain my balance.

Klifford hoisted me back into his arm simultaneously. "Losing his mind does not excuse his actions. In Burks's current state, he sees you as an enemy he must kill. So as far as we're concerned, he's our enemy." His indigo eyes searched for affirmation in mine.

I know... Sometimes it's kill or be killed. The only reason I'm unharmed is because Klifford is so strong. There's no telling what state I'd be in right now if Klifford wasn't here.

In the books, Sil had hesitated before he attacked Sirius, but did he pay the same courtesy to me? That, I did not know.

Wait, that's right. Sil can't be reasoned with right now. So why can't I just, like, make him not be our enemy anymore? If I could just snap him out of it...

Then it hit me.

Snap him out of it. That's it! My chances of success were...like, fifty-fifty. But there was this one time in the books where Sil returned to his normal self, even when he hadn't defeated everyone around him. Rather, there was one time where Super Sil was suddenly snapped back to his senses.

From that one scene, I was like, *Aha! So all those mysterious wipe-outs were Sil all along!* The circumstances here were different in many ways, but in the books, it was something Sirius did by chance. So I could do *the thing* on purpose to bring Sil back!

Probably. I hope. Like, a nine out of ten chance.

I knew how to do the thing. But...who would do it? *Hmmm... It's kind of a hardcore thing to do... Besides, I'll have the best chance at success if I do it myself.*

Okay. Decision made. Let's do this! I looked up at Klifford with determination. "Klifford. There's something I'd like to test out." And to carry out that test, I required a certain item. "Give me the dagger you hide in your sleeve."

I needed a weapon if I wanted to go all-out. And it happened that Klifford had just the right weapon. That was the hardness I'd felt on his arm. When I was telling him about my game of Spot the Weapon, he told me about the concealed daggers up his sleeve and in his boot— *this* was his sleeve dagger!

"You want...my dagger?" Klifford looked unusually suspicious. His brows were drawn together.

"Yes. And I want you to bring me as close to Sil as possible. Close enough for me to touch him... And make sure I'm safe from any outside attacks."

I hoped he wouldn't ask me why. If I told him my plan, Klifford would definitely be against it. And there was a huge chance that, as my bodyguard, he'd put a stop to it.

So I had to go harder. "This is my *command*...as your *Sovereign*," I whispered beneath the clamor of clashing steel.

For a couple seconds, my earnest eyes locked with his squinted indigos. Then Klifford nodded slightly and said, "Your wish is my command, Sovereign."

I removed my arms from around Klifford's neck and firmly gripped his dagger in my hand. I say *dagger*, but it was a little big for my hand. As daggers go, it was incredibly basic.

I pulled it from its sheath. The blade gleamed. It was immaculately maintained. Its blade looked pretty sharp. Noticing we were going to do something to Sil, the younger Adjutant left his fight with the other Adjutant and swung his blade at Klifford.

Dang, he's fast.

But OP-Klifford didn't even flinch as he countered, in spite of his encumbrance—me.

Including Klifford, there were at least three Adjutants in the room. In a word, they were *fast*. Fast, in every possible way. Each movement was smooth, like running water. Rather, if you tried to comprehend the entirety of the battlefield turned Sky Chamber, you wouldn't be able to follow all the inhuman movement. Seeing the big picture was utterly impossible.

My task at hand was to snap Sil out of his trance. I had to clear my mind of everything else.

Once I get close enough to Sil, I'll use this dagger, and... I ran the simulation in my mind on a loop. *When will I get my opening?* That question filled my head.

There was a shrill clanging of metal. Klifford's attack sent Sil's sword flying. Sil kicked himself backward, fumbling for another weapon. Klifford zoomed in on him.

There's my opening! I was close enough to touch Sil. *H-here goes nothing...* I held up my dagger. And then...I psyched myself up and slashed the palm of my left hand. It was a clean diagonal cut. *Urk!* I'd psyched myself up a little too much—the cut was much deeper than I intended.

The next thing I knew, someone was firmly gripping the wrist of my right hand—my dagger hand. That sent the blood from my left palm splashing onto that clean white uniform.

It was Klifford. A wave of emotions hit me. What was that blazing in his indigo eyes? *I-is he mad at me for deceiving him with my command? Sorry! B-but I had a good reason!*

"You said that my wish was your command, yes?" *It's do or die for me right now, Klifford!* "I promise you: I did not wound myself without reason."

"Aye..."

I wasn't sure if Klifford approved, but he released my wrist. Then he knocked down the volley of weapons that were flying at us.

I lowered my dagger and extended my bloody palm toward Sil. And unless I was mistaken, something in Sil would change when I cut myself.

When Sil saw my blood, he grunted, his eyes open wide. It was a dramatic change. *Yeah! The bleeding hurts like hell, but I really did make the right call!*

"Lord Sil." I touched his cheek with my bloodstained hand. The once-nimble young man was stiff as a statue. Then the strength drained from his body.

Here's a peek behind the curtain. In reality, this actually happens way in the future. In the latest volume of all the books I'd read in my past life, I was like, 90 percent sure that all the slayings had been committed by Super Sil himself. One time, Sirius got wounded when he was protecting Super Sil. When Sirius's blood hit his cheek, he passed out. And ohhh boy, that was an epic scene! For both Sil's trance story arc and for Boys Love romance!

In other words, it was *blood*! Super Sil's weakness was blood!

I revisited all the incidents where it looked like Sil maybe kinda slaughtered a bunch of people, and I realized that there wasn't a drop of blood shed. Though sometimes, Sil himself was wounded.

If he saw someone *else's* blood—if he was touched by it—he was snapped out of his trance. That was highly plausible.

But Sil never passed out at the sight of blood ordinarily. And he was in the presence of minor cuts and scrapes every day. This made me think the blood aversion was strictly a Super Sil thing. So I analyzed the things other characters had said, and there were some lines that implied that *royal blood* in particular held the key!

I remember I was kinda let down in my past life when I came to that realization. I mean, snapping back to his senses because it was *Sirius's* blood would have been so much more romantic!

But anyway…

Whether it's true or not, legend has it that Esfia's royal family has special blood, bestowed upon them from the Sky God or whatever. Anyway, that's why I had to be the one to test the theory! I, the princess! I'm royalty, of course!

I held up Sil as his muscles gave out. *Wait… Huh? In the books, Sil would completely pass out whenever he saw blood. But he's not…*

Sil weakly raised his head. But his eyes were vacant. No… They were staring at the blood on my hand.

"My *Sovereign*… Why…?" he murmured. Accusation colored his tone. *Sovereign…? Sil… Did you just say Sovereign?*

The image of a symbol thrashed about in my head. *Why Sil? No, wait, I shouldn't exactly think of Sil as Sil right now, should I?*

"Lord Sil?" I peered into his eyes. They opened wide again, just as they had when he first saw my blood.

"Your Majesty… My Sovereign." He reached out to me. His hand landed on my hair—the Lieche orchids threaded into it. He touched the blooms carefully, as if they were his precious treasure. Like he wanted to make sure they were really there.

And then...all the strength left Sil's body. I shook his shoulders, but there was no reaction. He really was unconscious now.

"Who's *Your Majesty*...?"

But I didn't have time to ponder it. Neutralizing Sil was one thing, but nothing else about our predicament had been resolved. The sound of swords—absent from my ears when I was focused on Sil—clanged on incessantly.

The leader-Adjutant had delayed dealing with me while Sil was in his trance. However! That worked out perfectly for him. He had a flaming aura—one that seemed excited to kill Sil and me both in one fell swoop. The younger Adjutant had a cooler aura—one that seemed to say *"Get away from Sil!"* —Actually, I take that back; he was going to separate us by force!

Hey, come on, we don't need to fight anymore, do we? I mean, going through the trouble of knocking everyone out would be such a bother! Now that Sil was (probably) back to normal, all we had to do was get out of there...

Let's beat a strategic retreat! Don't ask me how, though—I've got nothing!

My eyes darted to the entrance then.

What?

I saw a group of shadowy figures coming from the passageway. And for some reason, the redheaded man who Derek had indicated as our ally was the first to enter. When did he manage to step out of the room? But that question immediately flew out of my head.

The Sky Chamber was quickly filled with scores of armed soldiers. The redhead was leading someone inside. And that someone stepped forward, separating himself from the rows of soldiers.

I gasped. There was no mistaking it. I knew that silhouette. It was the man I would have begged to play the role of my fake boyfriend, were he unattached. I was so overcome with joy that I shamelessly shrieked.

"Uncle Dearest!"

The word *godsend* was made for moments like this. *Uncle Dearest! Uuuncle Deeearest! It's really youuu!*

I'm way too ecstatic to call him Duke Nightfellow! I think I see a halo around him!

"Sorry it took so long, Your Highness."

His smile... His voice... I forgot where I was and what was happening, and I just swooned.

42

In my past life, I had a big sister—in other words, I was the youngest!

In Esfia, I had a big brother—Sirius. But Heir Dilemma aside, he wasn't the kind of big brother I could fight with, whine at, or snuggle up against for comfort. He wasn't anything like my big sister was to me.

As for my parents now—King Enoch and his husband, Edgar—they were quite different from the sort of typical parents you'd see in Japan. This was partly because, being a same-sex couple as was customary in Esfia, they were of no direct blood relation to me. But the main difference was a matter of social standing. For starters, the mere act of seeing them outside of dinner was an epic ordeal! C'mon, show some compassion for your *daughter*! Lookin' at *you*, Father!

So rather than my "parents," I saw them much more as "the king and his husband." And being born into such an environment as a princess, I couldn't keep hold of my younger-sibling disposition.

But there was yet another difference—the biggest difference of all. My reborn-self had Alec! My precious baby brother! Well, now I just *had* to be a reliable big sister for him!

Still... When you compare my past life with my current one, my life as a younger sibling was longer. It wasn't like those memories had disappeared. Thus, I found someone who brings out the baby sister in me! It's Uncle Dearest! I even whined at him and annoyed him like a little sister!

And even though—after some tough introspection—I put some distance between us, he was already input into my brain as Guardian Angel Grown-up. Seeing him at a time like this especially made me feel so incredibly safe and relieved.

Well, now that Uncle Dearest is here, everything will be okay! Uh-oh, I think I'm gonna cry. The floodgates might still be full from my last cry. And all the tension I've been holding in my face and shoulders is long gone, besides.

And Sil was a man, let's not forget. He was heavy, holding him up for so long. I plopped right to the floor, with Sil still in my arms.

"We have the area surrounded. Lay down your weapons, and we shall spare your lives." Uncle Dearest's voice boomed from behind me, out through the Sky Chamber. "But if you resist, then we will take you by *force.*"

At his last word, the soldiers behind him menacingly readied their weapons. They moved as one body, disciplined and without a single hair out of place. I assumed this was House Nightfellow's private army, and I was sure it could hold its own, even against the Esfian Royal Army.

"Do you surrender, or don't you? Make your choice."

With the arrival of my guardian angel—Uncle Dearest—and his reinforcements, the tables had turned in the Sky Chamber. It took me a while to notice since I was too busy swooning over Uncle Dearest, but the intruders and their two Adjutants had stopped moving. And upon closer glance, the only members of their party who were still kickin' were the Adjutants. Everybody else seemed like they could barely stand on their own two feet.

No, I take that back. The Adjutant...the younger of the two. He has a coarse slash wound in his left arm. He probably got that from Klifford.

I checked Klifford—and sighed in relief. He was probably angry when he grabbed my wrist, but after that, he acted like his usual self. The blood on his white suit hadn't increased, either, as far as I could tell. He stood protectively in front of me as I held Sil on the ground. I couldn't see his face.

What about Derek and Rust...? I scanned the room. *They're both okay!*

They were right next to that…cenotaph. It was the spot where Sil and I used to be, before we moved. Derek and Rust were standing close to each other. There was a pile of intruders at their feet. I guess they teamed up.

Are they hurt? No… I don't think so. The blood on their clothes is enemy blood. I hope.

For some reason, Derek shot Uncle Dearest a scornful look—what a way to thank our lifesaver. And Rust was… Well, he was wearing a mask. But he was the one person who didn't even give the Sky Chamber's entrance a glance. He was looking down at the cenotaph…with the name Idéalia Esfia engraved on it.

So in spite of a couple concerns, all my allies were okay.

Yes! I did a little victory fist pump in my mind. My case of Uncle Dearest fever had mostly subsided, and the only two enemies who posed a clear threat were the two Adjutants. What's more, as powerful as Adjutants were, one of them was wounded. When faced with the huge army that Uncle Dearest had brought with him, surrender was definitely……*not what they were doooing?!*

Since I had been closely watching the Adjutants for a sign, even with his hood, I could tell the younger Adjutant exhaled sharply and gripped his sword hilt!

Wait a minute… Does Uncle Dearest know there are Adjutants among the intruders? I don't remember hearing that. But if the red-headed man is connected to Uncle Dearest, he's surely told him… You'd think he would.

I cried out at Uncle Dearest, "Duke Nightfellow! Those two men are Adjutants. Don't initiate an unnecessary fight!"

It was a nice idea and all, but how would Uncle Dearest know which "two men" I was talking about? *I* knew who they were, but I hadn't described them clearly to him. I was about to yell out "Addendum!" but before I could, Uncle Dearest answered promptly.

"Yes, Your Highness. I appreciate the warning." He narrowed his charcoal-gray eyes and smiled. Simultaneously, he signaled the red-headed man.

Uncle Dearest...isn't particularly surprised? Redheaded man, you are legit! He must've told Uncle Dearest about the Adjutants!

"I have the same opinion, Your Highness. I wish to avoid fighting an Adjutant as much as possible."

"Yes... Very wise of you." I nodded smugly. *We've gotta make the Adjutants surrender without a fight! That's the dream scenario! The one I totally just fumbled! But...how's he gonna manage it? I came here without a plan, but I trust Uncle Dearest! I just know he'll make it happen somehow!*

The younger Adjutant, who'd started to move when I called out to Uncle Dearest, froze still again the moment Uncle Dearest opened his mouth. He was probably waiting to see what Uncle Dearest's next move would be.

The redheaded man—who'd stepped out at Uncle Dearest's command—returned to the Sky Chamber. He was leading a girl by the hand. She looked about twelve years old. She had fluffy silver hair and eyes like emeralds.

She's crazy pretty! That baby blue dress made her look like a fairy, and it was definitely very *her.* Judging by her clothing, she was of the nobility...which made her a guest at the junior ball?

She shyly put a hand to her chest and slowly shook her head side to side. Her eyes clouded over. I felt something was amiss in her actions. Could it be...that she was blind?

"Um... Duke Nightfellow, are you certain? Is my...is my attendant really here? I smell...blood. Is Emilio wounded? Has...has something terrible happened?"

"Lady Turchen. Forgive me, but I do not know what your attendant looks like. Besides, he seems quite wary of me. Perhaps if you call out to him, he will answer you."

"All right..." Guided by the redheaded man, the girl took one step forward. If she took another step, there would be an intruder lying at her feet...

So I was right. She was blind. Without the redheaded man's guidance, she would have taken a second step forward as if there were nothing to obstruct her.

Why did Uncle Dearest bring her to a place like this…?

"Emilio? Are you there?"

I heard the sound of teeth grinding. It came from the younger Adjutant—the one in the hood.

"Yes… I am right here, my lady," the Adjutant—Emilio—answered.

The color returned to the girl's cheeks. "Emilio… Oh, thank goodness. You are…unharmed, I hope?"

There was no answer. The girl's cheeks once again lost their color. "What were you doing in here? Have you finished whatever it is you needed to do? Emilio?"

The Adjutant named Emilio still did not answer her. Uncle Dearest answered in his place.

"I think he has something rather difficult to tell you. Lady Turchen, I need to speak with Emilio right now. I hope you get a chance to speak with him later. For now…go wait for him elsewhere."

With a look of painful reluctance, the girl let the redheaded man lead her by the hand out of the Sky Chamber.

Lady Turchen… Turchen, as in *that* Turchen. As it was a historically significant place, the feudal lord of that land held the title of Lord Turchen. He wasn't a count. "The Lord of Turchen" was an independent noble title. That meant she wouldn't have been on the official guest list for this junior ball. But wouldn't the Lord of Turchen be back in his own domain—? *Oh! The Council of Feudal Lords!*

Then again, why would anybody bring a little girl to a place like this? This has nothing to do with her… Uncle Dearest! Well, I mean, it looks like she's that Adjutant's Sovereign, so maybe this does have something to do with her, but forget about that for a second—it's not okay to take her into a gruesome fight scene just because she can't see! She smelled blood, and I'm sure she sensed that something was off. She must have been terrified.

"Unc—"

"Piece of shit," Emilio grunted, throwing his sword down. My words "*Uncle Dearest?*" remained unspoken. The Adjutant, now unarmed and having surrendered, shot a fiery gaze of wrath at Uncle Dearest.

Meanwhile, Uncle Dearest's expression remained unchanged. "If you cannot choose between the life of your Sovereign and your mission, then you shouldn't have launched an attack. Now you are left with no choice but to abandon one or the other. Unable to make the choice, you left your Sovereign's side—without a plan—and pushed her into danger by coming in here... Adjutant. Your kind are indeed powerful, but if your enemy uses your Sovereign as a shield, you are weak even in the face of rookie soldiers. Much more so if your Sovereign is ignorant—the equivalent of an infant."

"............!" Emilio scowled at the duke.

"Direct your anger not at me but at yourself, Adjutant. Channel your fury into devotion for your Sovereign—keeping watch by her side every waking moment—and endowing your enemy no vulnerabilities to exploit."

Y-yikes. That's some pretty tough vocabulary. It's difficult to parse... Umm... So Lady Turchen—that pretty girl—is Emilio's Sovereign, but she doesn't know it... Is that why he called her ignorant? But can you really form a Sovereign-Adjutant connection in ignorance? What a mystery.

But let's say they *did* have an Adjutant-Sovereign bond—Uncle Dearest had the Sovereign girl in the palm of his hand.

So in other words...

"An Adjutant with a Sovereign taken hostage is powerless," the other Adjutant—the one with jet-black eyes—murmured. "When his eyes and limbs are bound, he cannot fight back. You're using the same tactic that *devil* once used on us Adjutants."

"That devil"?

"So that's why you bear a grudge against Esfia."

Wait... Uncle Dearest... Do you know who he's talking about?

"Not at all, Nightfellow. We think nothing of Esfia. *I* don't, at least.

After all, such a tactic doesn't work on an Adjutant without a Sovereign. Didn't you know? When we witnessed that *devil*'s deed, many of the Adjutants who survived adopted a new motto."

His hand moved. "Sovereigns...are bearers of doom!" Spitting out those words, the black-eyed Adjutant threw some weapons and retreated. His target was—Uncle Dearest!

His soldiers were nimble, but Derek got there first—deflecting the first projectile by throwing his sword. The second and third attacks were blocked by the soldiers. A group of soldiers mobilized to block his escape path.

But the Adjutant was headed in the opposite direction. His target was me. Or Sil? The moment Sil fell under his berserk trance, the dark Adjutant's mission had changed—from capturing Sil to killing him.

I tightened my hold on Sil.

"Protect Her Highness!" Uncle Dearest barked an order.

The Adjutant's eyes locked with mine. It wasn't Sil. His target was *me*.

An emboldened light filled his jet-black eyes. He had *not* given up his fight—nor was he ready to die. He was determined. Determined to escape.

He wasn't going to kill me. He had a better chance of escaping alive if he took the princess as a hostage. If he did that, Uncle Dearest might have to make his guards pull back.

As the Adjutant lunged toward me, he cursed loudly. Klifford had cut in from the side, blocking his path. And I wasn't just sitting there, either. I'd somehow managed to drag Sil off to the side.

Out of the corner of my eye, I caught a glimpse of Klifford and the Adjutant exchanging blows. *I shouldn't move—I might just get in their way.* I set my bottom down on the floor.

"Klifford! Capture him alive!"

This Adjutant *must* know something about Sil. And while, ordinarily, he would be the sort of opponent one would need to desperately lash out at just to have a chance at barely getting a hit in—I knew Klifford could beat him.

Klifford can take him alive. It's okay. I trust him.

"Understood, Your Highness." An audacious smirk formed on Klifford's lips.

"Capture me alive? You insult me!" The Adjutant's fierce onslaught began.

The soldiers were staying away from the fighting—from us. That was just how next-level both the Adjutant's and Klifford's fighting was. Even I knew that I should just stay still, lest I get in Klifford's way.

They were evenly matched—though Klifford was at a bit of a disadvantage. When this Adjutant had fought Emilio, he had been holding back a little, whether intentionally or not. And when Klifford had fought against Emilio, he had been backed up a little by Sil.

He had never confronted Klifford head-on, in earnest. But now the Adjutant *was* earnest—unleashing his superior battle prowess in full force against Klifford. In addition to his advantage in years, his position as leader suggested he was more skilled than Emilio, the other Adjutant.

He was fighting Klifford, but he was also trying to get away from him. His target was me, through and through. The Adjutant's prize was on the other side of Klifford. He could not capture me unless he defeated Klifford.

A terrible scenario flashed in my mind. An Adjutant is incapacitated if his Sovereign is taken hostage. What if the worst happened, and I was captured? If someone was cognizant of the fact that Klifford and I had a Sovereign-Adjutant bond, they would be able to stop Klifford from fighting.

But that wasn't all. In a way, I was indirectly commanding my Adjutant. That meant I could make Klifford fight on whichever side I was on, right? If I was to be taken hostage right then, I might be forced to command Klifford to fight Uncle Dearest's men...

A shrill clang echoed ominously. Klifford's sword flew in the air.

"Klifford!"

It was too far for him to reach. The Adjutant's blade was already swinging down at him, besides. I wanted to squeeze my eyes shut, but I forced them open.

Klifford twisted his upper body, lunged backward, and kicked something with his foot. It was a sword. The sword that Emilio had thrown aside. It leaped off the stone floor as if it were alive. Klifford caught it in his left hand.

And from that moment on…Klifford's movements changed drastically. He was still strong—that hadn't changed. But he was even stronger now than when he fought with a sword in his right hand. Sometimes when Klifford fought, his eyes would gleam like a savage beast's. If he unleashed the full extent of his barbarism—this is probably what it would look like.

"That man is poison."

For some reason, the words my father had said resurfaced in my mind.

He was too powerful—maybe that was what made him poison. Like a ferocious beast, lusting for blood, growling and overwhelming his prey—that was how he fought. It was beautiful but terrifying. It was mind-boggling. My throat was parched just watching him.

The fight was still raging on. But it was now clear who was going to win. The Adjutant was on full defense. It was taking everything in him just to parry the rapid succession of jabs. And the disarray of his movements born of this increased significantly.

And then, just as he did with Rust, Klifford thrust the tip of his sword at the Adjutant's neck. Last time, he'd stopped short of touching Rust's skin. But this time, he lunged with such force that I was surprised the Adjutant's head wasn't flying already. More than anything, the transformation in Klifford's fighting style suggested it.

With an agonizing moan, the Adjutant crumpled. Klifford threw the sword from his left hand back onto the stone floor. There wasn't so much as a scratch on the Adjutant's neck. After stopping short of cutting him, Klifford had knocked the Adjutant unconscious with the blunt end of his blade.

Silence filled the Sky Chamber—but not from the enemy's defeat. Klifford turned back to look at me. The fight was over, and there wasn't a single wound on his body—making my own bloodstain stand out all the more awkwardly on his white uniform.

Our eyes locked. And a cluster of wrinkles slowly formed between Klifford's eyebrows. The indigo in his tired eyes grew bolder. There were no traces of the savage spirit that had overtaken him during the fight. He was back to his usual bodyguard self. He picked up his own sword, returned it to its sheath, and walked over to me. I couldn't help but stare dumbly at him, wondering what he wanted.

"Your hands…" Klifford knelt before me and took my hands off Sil's shoulders.

He gently touched my right hand. It was then that I realized I was still holding the gloriously basic dagger. I wanted to drop it, but my fingers were frozen stiff over it, and it was really hard to let go. My veins were probably still full of adrenaline.

Oh! Why did it take me so long to notice?! Blackfeather… Where is it?

That was what should have been in my hand. I had no memory of dropping it, and I knew I had it in my hand when I ran up to Sil. If I had dropped it, it probably would have been when I was dodging Super Sil's sword.

As I lowered my clasped hand, I blinked myself out of my rambling thoughts. *Whoa…huh? That's…amazing.* As if under a spell, my fingers carefully removed themselves from the dagger's hilt, one by one. I tried opening my hand and making a fist. They moved—so easily that it was hard to believe they were previously frozen.

Klifford took the dagger and expertly cut the fabric of his white sleeve. "Allow me to tend to your hand. I can't perform anything beyond basic first aid, but I can stop the bleeding."

He took my left hand next, and without a word, he wrapped it with the fabric from his sleeve. And the cascade of dripping blood stopped!

"Thanks…"

Terrifyingly powerful as he was, he was still Klifford. *I'm so ashamed of myself. I let Father's cryptic words get to me, when I'd decided not to!*

I expected him to return my gratitude with "You needn't thank me, Your Highness," but instead—

"I am furious."

Uh... D-did I mishear him, maybe? "I'm sorry. What did you just say?"

"I'm terribly furious."

S-so I didn't mishear him. He even added a "terribly" this time.

Well, *that* just took a turn for the worse!

Sil, His Excellency, and the Redheaded Man

It was the first time Duke Nightfellow had requested to see me by name.

"Good evening, Duke Nightfellow. It is indeed an honor. I am forever in your son's debt." I somehow managed a greeting.

"I am pleased to hear it."

"Don't you think it's a bit harsh to refer to me as your *sorry excuse for a son*, Father?"

The duke's gaze traveled from me to Derek. He thoughtfully stroked his chin and nodded. "Perhaps *foolish son* would have been more apt."

"Er... But that carries the same meaning." Derek sighed.

While Derek was a longtime friend of mine, I could count the number of times I'd spoken with his father on one hand. And Sirius was always with me, besides. So this was not only the first time I was personally invited to chat with Duke Nightfellow; it was the first time I saw him banter with his son.

"So, foolish son, about the matter of your marriage," the duke said abruptly, as if he was discussing the weather.

Derek spat out the wine he'd received from a server.

"Are you all right, son?"

"Father... I thought I made my refusal clear."

"And I did say no on your behalf, of course."

"Then why...?"

"The news of Octavia's secret romance seems to have inspired her to ask again. *Especially* after having seen your opening dance with Her Highness. Perhaps it would be more correct to say it was *because* of the dance?"

Duke Nightfellow turned his attention toward a middle-aged nobleman and a young lady who appeared to be his daughter. The nobleman had a familiar face—it was the face that was pounded into my head as someone I must remember. It was a count who was among Sirius's allies.

"It seems she doesn't mind the idea of you having a male lover on the side."

The duke's casual remark made me feel uneasy. It was an area in which I still lacked self-confidence. Even though, logically, I understood a potential love affair, my heart threatened to reject it. And I felt like that part of me was being pestered.

Derek stole a glance at me, then he answered, "I have no such thing."

"She made a point to inquire about your potential lover—don't take that lightly. I doubt she'll give up on you unless she hears a *no* directly from your lips."

"Fine... I understand, Father." Derek sighed in defeat. "Sorry, Sil, but I have to leave for a bit. Remember what I told you earlier. There's no telling who's watching. Stay vigilant—don't let your guard down."

"I'll be careful; I promise."

Leaving me with that final warning, he walked away. As we watched his back disappear into the crowd, his father chuckled.

"It feels strange to say this as his father, but Derek is like a mother to you, Burks."

The unease in my heart lingered. It took a little longer to answer him than I would have liked. "I think...it's because I am unreliable. Your son is very attentive and kind."

"As the heir to my house, my son is a little too naive for my liking. He's too easily swayed by emotion."

"I see that as a virtue, Your Grace."

"From a different perspective, I suppose you're right, Burks. At times, I envy my son. And at other times, I find him utterly frustrating."

Light or shadow—this was a phrase often attributed to Duke Leif Nightfellow. Opinions of the duke's character were polar opposites, depending on whom you asked. He was a merciful man who cared for his subjects. He was also a devil, who shed neither blood nor tears.

It was hard to believe both descriptions belonged to the same man. But this did not mean that his personality was bankrupt. No, the answer was much simpler than that: He was kind to his friends, ruthless to his enemies. Whichever side you sat on would determine whether you saw the duke as light or shadow.

As for me… I wasn't certain which side I was on yet. I was on neither side, to be honest. Just like Derek was consistently neutral in Octavia's eyes, I was neutral in the duke of Nightfellow's eyes. I was neither welcomed nor shunned…

And even a "neutral" social standing meant completely different things to the duke and his son. Of course, I felt no animosity from the man. But that was only because—

"Duke Nightfellow, so good to see you here! I would love to pay my respects," one of the party guests called out, approaching us. A small crowd of people saw their opening and followed him. There were quite a few people who wished to make a connection with Duke Nightfellow.

The duke began to walk off with the small crowd. "Well, good-bye, Lord Burks. See you *soon*."

See me…soon?

The casual pleasantry tugging on my conscience, I abruptly righted myself from bowing. But Duke Nightfellow was no longer looking my way.

Now that I was away from Derek and his father, I was back at the starting gate.

I was alone. My skin tingled, sensing the prying eyes of the room following my every move. Somebody in that room might be my birth mother or father…or someone connected to them.

Stay sharp. Don't let your guard down. You begged Princess Octavia to help you, and she was kind enough to oblige. You can't leave until you get the answers you came here for.

But…I've lost my nerve. I stopped in my tracks, sensing the stares all around me, and walked to the corner of the hall. From there, I got a good look at the guests.

I looked and looked… But in my heart, I knew my birth parents were not in sight. Neither was there any sign of the mysterious someone who'd given me the information about them.

Are they waiting for me to be alone? Maybe I should leave the main hall and go someplace more secluded.

If I was going to do that, now was the time. Derek's watchful eye was no longer on me. If I did find a vital clue and managed to meet my birth parents, that would be great and all… But what if I ran into a trap instead? If it was one against one, I'd have a good chance, but if I was attacked by a mob, would I be able to hold my own against them? If I was to relocate to a secluded place, I couldn't do so until I was certain my parents and the one who led me to them were safe.

Several minutes passed as I thought long and hard about it. Then I heard the sound of something hitting the ground nearby. I looked toward the source of the sound—to my right. It was a walking stick. It was wooden and very well-made. A girl in a pale blue dress was trying to pick it up, but her hands weren't quite touching it.

"Allow me," I said, approaching her. I picked up the walking stick and handed it to her. When she touched it, she sighed in relief, her pale little hands gripping it tight.

"Thank you!" She smiled sweetly. She was looking right at me—my voice probably clued her in to where I was. But her emerald-green eyes did not see me. She was about eleven or twelve years old.

Even assuming she is a guest, isn't she a bit young to be here alone? Most children her age who attended junior balls were accompanied by their parents or elder brothers. Even if they were the one invited, they always took a chaperone... At least that's how it usually was.

"Where is your chaperone, little girl? Shall I help you find them?"

The girl looked up at me coyly, her downy silver hair shaking as she laughed. "Are you worried about me? That's very kind of you. But don't worry, I have my attendant with me. He's off getting me a drink right now, so I am staying here until his return."

"Well, that's good to hear." *But maybe I should stay with her until her attendant comes back.*

"So um... My name is Liliciana. What's your name?"

At junior balls, it's customary to omit one's surname when one wishes to carry on a casual conversation disregarding social status. It's similar to wearing masks at a masquerade ball.

"I'm Sil."

"Nice to meet you, Lord Sil!" Liliciana's face lit up. For better or worse, the name Sil was well-known throughout the royal capital— throughout noble circles in general. Even girls Liliciana's age were rather knowledgeable on who I was. But Liliciana didn't seem to have heard of me.

Maybe she was the daughter of a nobleman from far away who came to attend the Council of Feudal Lords. That would explain her ignorance on current royal gossip. I laughed silently, realizing that a part of me was grateful for her ignorance. *Come on, Sil... You can't be like this.*

"Lord Sil, do you attend junior balls like this one often?"

"I...would like to attend them more often, I suppose. What about you, Liliciana?"

"This is my first junior ball. I'm quite enjoying myself—even though I can't see anything, I can feel the festivity in the air. I cannot thank Duke Nightfellow enough for his kindness."

"Duke Nightfellow, you say?"

Liliciana nodded. "Yes. There was a cancellation in his party, so he kindly sent me an invitation to join him yesterday."

A cancellation? Yesterday? So suddenly?

If anything, news of Octavia attending the junior ball surely had crowds of people kicking at his door begging for an invitation.

"Oh!" Liliciana suddenly gasped. She moved her walking stick and took an urgent step forward.

"Liliciana?"

"I hear footsteps—it's my attendant. He's come to fetch me."

"Lili—" I chased after her, thinking it would be best if I could at least make sure she was safely back in her attendant's care before I moved on. And no sooner did I take one step than—

"Oops! Pardon me," a voice apologized insincerely as a drink splashed on my clothes. The collider was a redheaded man, glass in hand. He was slender and wearing a mask that matched the color of his hair. Socializing in a mask... That was an event held in the pleasaunce hall at this junior ball tonight. Some guests elected to keep their masks on outside the pleasaunce hall as well as inside. This man was one of them.

The splashed liquor on my clothes smelled like grape wine, but it was rather colorless. It must have been white wine.

When the masked man saw my wine-soaked suit, he made such an exaggerated gasp that I could see it through the mask. "Oh, dear. I wasn't looking where I was going... Please, let me make it up to you with a change of clothes, *Lord Sil Burks.*"

It was probably an act of spite. Unless...it was someone's way of trying to make contact with me...?

I searched for Liliciana with my eyes. She was with a young man— he was probably her attendant. There was a clear sense of trust in her smile as she spoke with him.

Liliciana is in safe hands. So...what do I do now?

"Well, if that was enough to convince you to come with me without question, you'd be pretty dim-witted, now, wouldn't you?" The red-headed man's tone of voice quickly changed into a secretive murmur. He pretended to dab up the spilled wine off my jacket as he whispered, "I'm a messenger of Duke Nightfellow. His Excellency made a point to tell you he would see you *soon*, didn't he?"

Yes…he did. But when the duke and I parted ways, this man wasn't in our general vicinity. Was he really a messenger of the duke? Or did another party guest tell him about our conversation so he could exploit it?

The young man stepped away from me, making a show of waving his wet handkerchief. "That was all I could clean with a handkerchief. I do think it would be best if you changed clothes. Please, won't you let me make it up to you?"

After a brief pause, I nodded in agreement. "Thank you. I kindly accept your offer."

The redheaded man took me to a room that was actually Paradise in the Sky's men's dressing room. Nobody would find it strange if I spilled wine on my suit and went there to change. But the man who was in there waiting for me… Now, *that* was strange. He was the sort of person who would have used one of the rooms reserved for high-ranking noblemen if he needed to change clothes. A part of me still couldn't believe what I saw before me.

"Hello, Lord Burks. Come on in."

"Thank you…for the invitation, Your Grace."

What's more, why did he use this method to summon me? The main hall should be more than sufficient for that purpose. Sitting across from me, smiling warmly with black hair and charcoal-gray eyes— was Duke Nightfellow.

"See? I wasn't lying when I said His Excellency wanted to speak with you," said a playful voice. It was the masked redheaded man. "Oh, and you needn't make my acquaintance—just think of me as an inconsequential bystander."

"I think you might have phrased that better…" Duke Nightfellow sighed heavily. This action reminded me exactly of Derek, right down to the look on his face. Like father like son. The only difference was… if Derek summoned me in this manner, I wouldn't feel any suspicion. I can't say I trusted his father as much.

"Oh, but isn't what I said technically true, Your Excellency? Oh! That's right, I have a story for you! I asked Princess Octavia's bodyguard to dance in the pleasaunce hall, and he turned me down!"

"*Boy...* What the hell do you think you're doing?"

"Well, I was sweating bullets out there! I was scared that my cover as a purehearted party guest would be blown, and my mission would be in jeopardy, you see. Oooh, it was dreadfully scary. I had not a single weapon on me! To look at me, anyone would think I'm a weak and delicate little flower of a nobleman. Then, when I happened to dance with Her Highness by chance soon after, oh, my heart was a nervous flutter in my mouth! Her Highness almost stepped on my foot! Do you suppose that was her way of warning me to get my act together? What do you think, Your Excellency?"

"You danced with her *by chance*? You've been interpreting my commands way too liberally, my boy."

"Oh, but Your *Excellency*! I am seeking out a fated encounter. Both ladies and gentlemen are welcome, so long as they are beautiful! Beautiful people are humankind's greatest treasure!"

"Baldo would cry if he heard you say that..."

"Isn't my dear father taking command of the garden guards at the moment? Yes, perhaps he would race over here to give me a stern talking—yeah, no, he wouldn't. Well, I do not wish to turn out like him anyway. Straight shooter like that. It's *your* fault he's like that, Your Excellency."

"Baldo is fine just the way he is. Everybody has their own unique role to play."

"Is that why you've given me this role? I'm fine with it, actually. Alllrighty then, Burksie, do you feel all nice and relaxed now? Do ya?"

I gulped. Then I said, "Duke Nightfellow—why did you summon me to speak with you alone like this? Is it...a matter you don't want Derek overhearing?" At the time, my mind was preoccupied, so I didn't think much of it. But now that I was in here, this all felt like it was something Duke Nightfellow had orchestrated.

"My son is friends with you. He's too close—emotionally. If he was to find out what I'm about to command of you, he would surely try to interfere. That's why I made sure the two of you were separated."

What he's about to command of me…? "Do you have a command for me?"

"I do, but first, I'll need to make certain of a few things. Why did you attend this junior ball alone?"

That was a secret I'd only shared with Octavia. The duke seemed unperturbed by my silence and continued, "Did you come here because you'd received some intelligence?"

I held my breath and stared hard at the duke. *Was it him? Was he the one who sent me the tip that my birth parents would be at Countess Reddington's junior ball?*

The duke quietly shook his head in the negative. "Let me clarify, so that you will not misunderstand. I do not know the contents of that intelligence. However, I did make arrangements so that intelligence would reach you."

"It was you…who sent it to me?" That begged the question, "Do you know *who* was the source of that intelligence?"

"Just a type of rat…"

"A…rat?"

"Let's just say, this is a certain dissident who is difficult to denounce. Someone who is causing Esfia direct harm. There are many ways I could describe this individual, but it is an enemy who must be exterminated—that much is clear. If we leave this rat be, it will inter-act with other rats, and they'll multiply, their nests carpeting the land. Unless we demolish the main nest, any efforts to clear up the other nests will only produce meager outcomes. However, this rat seldom leaves its nest—it's quite vexing."

"This rat… Has it crawled out of its nest in an attempt to connect with me?"

The duke smiled softly and nodded, as if I were his student and he was proud of me for answering him correctly. But his smile quickly vanished. "For a time, I considered that *you* might be one of those rats, Mr. Burks."

Like Derek, the duke's demeanor and tone of voice were quite calm and gentle. But it was then that I noticed the peaceful aura that surrounded him was purely an illusion created by the gentle look in his eyes. When the manufactured kindness vanished, all that remained were the chiseled face of a statue and a demeanor as sharp as ice.

A chill surged through my veins.

"The royal family, bewitched by lust, tips the kingdom in someone else's favor—what if, for the sake of argument, a rat commanded you to become lovers with Prince Sirius? The rat could send the kingdom into disarray through His Highness."

For an instant, a flash of rage consumed my brain. "Sirius is not so foolish. He would never bend the law of the land out of affection for me."

"Well... I hope you're right."

I clenched my fists. My rebuke didn't seem to faze Duke Nightfellow one bit. It was a fact that made my blood boil. "Is *that* why you summoned me here, my lord? To determine whether I was one of these *rats* of whom you speak?"

"Your Excellency, you shouldn't tease Burksie so. Be kind to beauty!" the redheaded man cut in. "Fear not, Burksie, all doubts about you have been washed away, squeaky-clean! *Light or shadow?* Light, I say. The baddies are just after *you*, Burskie; it's very simple, really. That's why Prince Sirius has been so hypervigilant."

If this was all true, then the suspicions of *me* being the dissident in question...were cleared?

A chuckle escaped Duke Nightfellow's mouth. "Prince Sirius is keeping a vigilant watch over you. He never lets anything that might be troublesome or suspicious come your way. He protects you so obsessively that even if a rat were to scatter crumbs as bait, there would be no birds to snatch it up."

So the one who gave me the intelligence about my birth parents... That was probably an underling of the *rat* of whom the duke spoke. We could capture this underling, but this would not lead us to the main rat's nest. So rather than capture them—the duke had opted for exposing their plot.

"My lord... Am I to understand that you offered a helping hand to the rat?"

"They don't show their scrawny, hairless tails so easily. Yet they seem to have taken a liking to you, Mr. Burks. And attending this junior ball was a decision you made on your own. It makes me wonder, what in that intelligence could have possibly caused you to act so rashly? Still—what's most crucial to me is this: You are to be the bait that will lure our rat out of hiding."

I just stood there, watching the door close in front of me. The duke had left the room, leaving me alone with the redheaded man.

My conversation with Duke Nightfellow...was surprisingly short. And it wasn't conversation so much as it was an interrogation. The duke was seeking my cooperation. He wanted me to be the bait that would lure rats into a trap. And while the rats were distracted by the bait—me—the duke would capture them. Sirius would not have let me do it if he knew. And Derek would have strongly opposed the idea. That's why the duke had asked me privately.

And there was one more thing—

"With definitive proof, His Majesty the King will have no choice but to take action."

That was something the duke had said during our little chat. From the way he said it, it sounded like the king didn't want to take action—that he wanted to let the dissident roam free.

And the parting words we exchanged as the duke left the room still resonated in my head.

"What if I refuse to cooperate with your plan, my lord? What will happen to me?"

"As far as you're concerned, you will return to the junior ball, have a good time, then return home. The choice is yours to make, Mr. Burks. Have a good evening."

Until that moment, I hadn't let myself fully trust him. But did this mean I could take everything he'd said at face value? Maybe it really *was* Duke Nightfellow who had enticed me to attend the junior ball. And maybe *he* was the one who was after me. But if that was the case, the moment I set foot in that room, he could have burned me, boiled me, or disposed of me any way he pleased. He could have captured me, too.

Yet here I am. A free man.

The choice at hand was whether I should accept Duke Nightfellow's mission or reject it. I could walk out of this room right now if I wanted to. I doubt the redheaded man would try to stop me. Which meant—

I looked at the redheaded man. "May I ask you a question?"

"Yes, yes, of course! If it's a question I can answer, then I shall," the redheaded man answered flippantly—yet he showed no sign of removing his mask.

According to the duke, this man was one of his underlings. What's more, he was a spy who had successfully infiltrated the rats' network. He certainly didn't look like a spy to me. But then again, *that* was proof that he could successfully infiltrate any organization.

"If I don't cooperate with your plan, and I return to the junior ball… what will happen to the rats?"

"The ones who wish to abduct Princess Octavia will be caught, I'll wager."

"Huh?"

"Oh, haven't you heard? Yes, the princess's appearance at this junior ball sure has made both our tasks much easier."

"Is Princess Octavia in danger? Then we must catch her abductors at once!" I grabbed the man's shirt collar.

"Urk! My biggest assets are my silver tongue and running speed! Followed closely by dancing! I am against violence."

"Oh… Pardon me." I quickly released him.

"You have quite a temper beneath that delicate exterior, Burksie. Are we bloodthirsty, mayhaps?"

"It would be more ridiculous *not* to lose my temper! Princess Octavia is in danger!"

The redheaded man seemed a bit uncomfortable. "Ah, don't worry about her. My dear father—His Excellency's confidant is handling that little problem. Unlike me, he's a master of the sword. I assure you, no harm will come to Her Highness. Besides, she's already got a terrifying ally on her side."

"Right… Sir Alderton…"

"That's the one! Her esteemed bodyguard. If we're talking who's the most at risk here, don't *you* win that contest, Burksie?"

"You still haven't answered my question. If I don't help you lure the rats who are after me out of hiding, what will happen?"

If I decided to cooperate, this man would take me to the rats—traitors who might know something about who I really am.

"Well, I'm just a lowly underling… But I think they'll probably pull back. See, normally, if His Excellency steps into the spotlight, the rats won't go for the bait, no matter how tasty it looks."

"What do you mean…?"

"Well, hmmm… Say, Burksie, do you think thieves would go out of their way to rob a heavily guarded venue? They wouldn't, of course. Too much work. Easy is best. So if you wish to make your event attractive to thieves, make it look like you've grossly underestimated them. That's why Countess Reddington is hosting this junior ball. In fact, the countess is anything but helpless. But they've got preconceived notions about ladies of the nobility. They assume that a junior ball hosted by a woman will be a picnic to assault. If you need proof of that, look no further than the gullible rats who are after Princess Octavia."

The redhead paused, tilted his head, and scratched the back of it. "It's just—I'm doing my best here, but the rats who are after you—oh, that's the group I'm undercover with—they don't let preconceived notions fool them. His Excellency's presence here alone is enough to tip them off that this place is heavily guarded. It's just, when *you* showed up at the junior ball, Burksie, they sorta decided to proceed with their plan anyway. Also, there's this place to consider."

"What about this place?"

"Our boys seem awfully knowledgeable about Paradise in the Sky. I get the feeling His Excellency picked up on that... So he thought if he gift wrapped a Burksie for them, that would make it all the more appealing, maybe?"

"Um... I don't quite follow..."

"Hmmm... How's this? If you want to lure rats out of their nest, Paradise in the Sky is an irresistible stage setting!"

"Oh, I think I understand now. In other words, tonight is the perfect opportunity for you to catch the rats?"

"You've got it."

The more I learned, the more I was inclined to say *"No thanks."* My refusal was practically set in stone.

"But let me tell you what I think," the redhead said, soberly looking at me and folding his arms. "As you heard me say earlier, I believe that beautiful people are humankind's greatest treasure."

"Yeah...?" I sighed warily. *I thought he was going to lecture me into cooperating—what the hell is he playing at?*

"Be they ladies or gentlemen, I don't really care what's on the inside as long as they've got pretty faces. Y'know how we desire what we are not?"

"Huh? Oh, I don't think you're—"

"Stop right there, sweetie, I don't need your pity. I promise you: I'm not much to look at without my mask. Well, I guess I'm...okay? I have mastered the art of exuding an air of beauty. Well anyway, what I mean to say is: You're a beauty, Burksie, so I like you."

A look of utter suspicion filled my eyes. Even if he was sincere, I was not at all flattered by his compliment.

"So a word of advice! I think it's best you spur His Excellency's proposal."

"Yeah, but I—" *Wait, what did he say?*

"Look, Burksie, if I take you back to the rats' nest, I can't guarantee your safety. My primary objective isn't to protect you. It's to find out where they're gathering tonight and contact His Excellency. If the worst happens, I plan on escaping and saving myself. His Excellency won't needlessly mobilize the troops to save little ol' me. Well, if it's Princess Octavia who needs saving, that's another story. Anyway, you shouldn't commit to this lightly—that's all I'm saying."

"Is it...that dangerous?"

"Um... You might die?"

In that case... This makes the duke's story all the more credible. At the very least, if I say yes, I'll be able to meet face-to-face with the people who are after me. They'll also believe I completely fell for their trap. And I'll also have an ally among them.

"I'm sure you're not too keen on the idea of dying. And I'd be a tad upset to lose a very important pretty person. So I suggest you stay out of this one."

"No... I'm coming with you."

"Excuse me?"

"I will cooperate with Duke Nightfellow."

"You mean...you'll be the bait? Well, not *bait* bait; it's technically *you* they're after."

"So it seems." I sighed.

I'd like to know the reason why they're after me just as much as the duke. Especially if that reason is somehow connected with my origins. If I lean on Sirius all the time...if I stay in his protective embrace forever... I'll never be able to grow.

"Um, do you understand the subtext of what I'm saying? His Excellency isn't gonna, like, jump in and save you just in the nick of time, you know? Saying yes means you acknowledge that. And even if you decide to go back to the junior ball and have a good time, I doubt His Excellency will tease you about it a few days from now. His Excellency is actually a pretty cool guy in that regard! Well, then again, sometimes he's *too cool*—to the point of being terrifying—and I really am so, *so* glad that Lord Derek didn't inherit *that* from his father. He takes after his mother that way. Even if it's a conflict of interest, Lord Derek always puts his friends first. He would never cast you aside without warning."

I interrupted the redhead's verbal barrage. "Um... I get the impression that you *don't* want me to cooperate? But wouldn't that make your task that much easier to carry out?"

"Well, yes... But I'm just so kind to beautiful people, you see!" he cried, smiling and giving me a thumbs-up.

My gaze was once again filled with suspicion. For a moment, I was consumed with the urge to snap his thumb in two.

"Take your time to make your decision. If you have any other questions, I'll gladly answer them."

Any other questions...

"Could you give me the full details of your plan? That would make my job easier, for one."

"Oh! Actually, I don't know," he answered, flapping his hand.

I doubted my ears for a moment. "You...don't know?"

"Nope."

This doesn't make sense.

"I think the only person who knows the whole story is His Excellency, maybe? I just know maybe ten percent of the plan. Wait, I lie. More like *thirty* percent."

"So you're saying the duke doesn't trust anybody?"

"I'm not so sure... From the role he gave me, I feel like his trust for me is absolute? The fact of the matter is: If he found out one of his own was a traitor, he'd flush us all out as enemies. Sometimes that's what it means to be a person in power."

"Don't you ever get...insecure about that?"

"Not really? His Excellency has the whole plan in his head anyway—all I need to do is be his eyes and his hands and move as he instructs me. His Excellency assigns a number to everything. If all those numbers fall into place, he'll reach the sum in his brain. Even if his numbers were off, His Excellency can simply correct them and amend his commands to us. On principle, His Excellency's actions are never in vain."

His actions are never in vain—

An image of Liliciana, the girl I met earlier, popped into my mind.

She wasn't supposed to attend this junior ball—Duke Nightfellow invited her at the last minute. He must have had intentions only he knew.

"Well, as someone who serves under His Excellency, all of this is second nature to me. His Excellency merely explicitly divides his level of trust among us. I mean, if I knew *everything* about the plan, and the enemy tortured me, I'd definitely sing. But if I don't know anything, then I can't. Now, about your last question, I think His Excellency did tell you everything you needed to know."

"Oh, I see…"

"So you're still fine with being our bait?"

"I am." I nodded.

"Oooh. Wait a minute, Burksie, don't tell me you *wanna* see the rats?"

That was a question I couldn't answer. So I asked him a question back. "I have one final question."

"Sure thing! What is it?"

"I believe Duke Nightfellow is at the center of this plan. But myself aside, Princess Octavia… Even though you say she is in very little danger, she *is* still being targeted, isn't she? If you know this to be fact, then shouldn't we tell His Majesty and mobilize the royal army?"

"Wellll… That probably won't work."

I figured he would evade my question. What I really wanted to know was: Why was a duke mobilized and not the entire kingdom?

But I was not expecting the answer he gave me. "His Majesty could see to it that Princess Octavia is protected, but that is all. He would not assist in the rat extermination."

I held my breath. "……Why?"

"See, when you work under His Excellency, you see things. Things you'd be better off not seeing. And the way I see it, His Majesty hates his kingdom. He hates the kingdom he rules over."

"But—" I was gutted. *That can't be… It just can't. His Majesty is a great king.*

"Oh dear, was that sacrilegious of me? Are you gonna tell Sirius?"

There's no way I can tell him.

"The former king was known to be quite a lazy fellow. And Esfia still functioned just fine, but he was completely different from the crown prince at the time—His Majesty the King. He's Sirius's father, all right. The spitting image. Oh, wait, he's not his father by blood, is he? Well, they are both not only beautiful but prodigious, what's more."

"Um, what exactly are you trying to say?"

"In a nutshell, he's not at all who he was when he was the crown prince. Ever since his enthronement, he's become a wonderful king at a glance, but he keeps making choices that weaken Esfia."

"Could you maybe...give me a specific example of this?"

"If you want something recent... Oh, I know! Take that war with the Saza Church a little while ago. His Majesty could have stopped that war before it even started...yet he waited. Like he was mulling something over... And he kept waiting, until the thread of tension snapped and all-out war erupted."

That war had ended with Esfia's victory. A grand celebration was held in the royal capital.

"The only reason nobody considered the war problematic was because, in the end, Esfia won. And Esfia suffered little damages as a result of the war."

There was nothing I could say in response. I wasn't exactly familiar with our current geopolitical situation.

"Look, Burksie, as Prince Sirius's future groom, you must be mindful of what agreeing to this mission means. You might die tonight. And if you do die, please don't curse me."

"Could you please not plan my funeral while I'm standing right here?"

"Any last words?"

"Shut up."

"Oops! Burskie, are you a bad boy now?"

I felt the pent-up tension suddenly leave my body. "Um... Could you please stop calling me Burksie?"

"Aw, I don't wanna." Suddenly, the redhead's entire atmosphere changed. "All joking aside, if you want to return to the junior ball, this is your last chance. Are you sure you want to agree to His Excellency's mission? Are you sure, Lord Burks?"

I gave him a firm nod in reply.

Pain shot through my neck. I clamped a hand over it, but I was too late.

I ripped off my blindfold.

And when I opened my eyes, I saw blue.

Blue—

I'm in a blue room... Am I still in the Sky Chamber?

But that's impossible. We walked so far.

I couldn't organize my thoughts.

I waved my hand, and it touched something. It was stone...a gravestone. There was writing carved into it.

—Idéalia Esfia?

I don't know that name.

"My Sovereign."

I...do know that name? No, I don't know it.

I shook my head.

The redheaded man had tricked me and taken me prisoner in the Sky Chamber.

I was blindfolded. Other men joined the redheaded man. Then we walked. We walked until we arrived here.

Somebody commended the redheaded man... Then I was hit by... something?

I didn't even get a chance to ask them about my birth parents.

I fell to my knees. I wanted to stand, but I couldn't. My limbs wouldn't obey me.

"It's not poison. You'll lose consciousness for a while," a man said.

I'll lose consciousness? No... I can't.

I'd much rather be poisoned.

Losing consciousness was more terrifying than dying. I always feared it, ever since I was a little boy. I always felt like something—something unknown to me—was rearing its ugly head.

Don't let it happen. Stay awake. I'm terrified.

It was exactly the same when my savior rescued me.

If he hadn't come...then all those people around me would've been...
I would have...

"Nothing will happen to you."

With the voice, a sword casually swung above me. It was sheathed. If I reached out, I could touch it...

But what for? No, don't think. Don't question it. Just grab the sword...

"Nothing will happen to you, as long as you aren't the existence we fear."

What if I am...the existence you fear? My throat was dry—my lips only formed the words—but the man still answered.

"Then we'll kill you. Don't curse us... Curse your parents who broke the ultimate taboo. Whatever the reason, a Sovereign and an Adjutant should have *never*—"

Before I could hear the rest of the man's sentence, I fell unconscious.

43

I—I guess apologizing would be a good start. Yeah. Let's do that. Apology time!

Yes. Ask for forgiveness...

But I stopped myself right there.

If I apologized, wouldn't Klifford's status as my underling force him to forgive me without question? That would only give us a superficial resolution to the problem.

Besides, it's kind of weird that I have no idea why Klifford is even angry!

Let's say it's something I did. I guess it would have to be how I sorta deceived him with that command. Or was it because I slashed my own hand? Was it the wound itself? Or was it the fact that I'd used Klifford's dagger to harm myself?

A-any of those scenarios check out, really. Could be all of them...

If it was some other reason I wasn't even thinking of, then I give up. But I got the feeling it would behoove me to acquaint myself with the finer points of Klifford's temper. So I could avoid making him lose it again!

What he'd just said—*"I'm terribly furious"*—hung in the air as I stared down at my bandaged left hand. It was about time I mustered up the courage to finally look up. But... Well... It would take a lot of courage to look Klifford in the eye, you know? *You'd* want to look away as soon as possible, and you know it!

B-be brave, Octavia. Be brave! First, find out why he's angry!

"Klifford—are you by any chance ambidextrous?"

Of course. Of course that's what flew out of my mouth.

I did manage to look up just a *little*... But then I choked! That was not a suitable thing to say in this kind of conversation. It wasn't! Curious though I was about his fighting style earlier!

"No... I am right-handed. I can sword fight with both, however. I adjust my fighting style to match the situation." He answered my question normally. I couldn't get a read on his emotions at all.

"Ah, I see..." *F-fine, I'll just keep talking and steer the conversation where it needs to go.* "Does this mean your left hand is more skilled at the sword?"

"When I use my right hand, all weapons feel far too comfortable to me."

"*Too* comfortable, you say?"

"I forget to adjust my fighting style."

Adjust his fighting style... I was the one who had commanded him to capture the Adjutant alive. The fight he just had with the Adjutant... Could it be...?

"Did you toss aside your sword on purpose?"

"Yes," Klifford answered calmly. "I was worried that if I fought with my own sword, I would mortally wound my opponent."

So even though he had determined fighting that Adjutant with his good sword in his left hand would have been advisable, he swapped out his weapon with an unfamiliar one in order to carry out my command...

This made one thing clear: During that epic, mind-blowing battle... Klifford was ridiculously calm.

And...he's still calm right now, isn't he?

I didn't sense any anger in his tone, and he seemed composed. But that didn't change the fact that he was terribly furious—he said what he said.

"Were you furious...with me?" I asked, forcing myself to look up at him.

I was met with a pair of indigo eyes, deeper and darker than ever. "With you...and with myself, Your Highness."

He's furious with himself?

For a moment, Klifford's gaze shifted to the unconscious Sil. "Your Highness... Do you cherish Burks?"

"Yes... He'll become my family in the future, after all."

But that wasn't all. Sil was the hero of *The Noble King*. I shared his joys and his sorrows as I read his story. I know that the world I'm in now is not the world of *The Noble King* as written. And since this world was not the same as *The Noble King*, neither were the people in it...

But in personality and in physical appearance, Sil was exactly as I had imagined him. Even though to me as Octavia, he represented a problem in my future that I would have to tackle, once I actually talked to him, I couldn't hate him. And I was desperate that he not hate me.

"I do not wish for him to be needlessly harmed."

"You do not wish for Burks to be needlessly harmed, yet you pay no mind to harming yourself?"

"You misunderstand... I only did what needed to be done."

As it turned out, spilling my own blood did snap Sil out of his trance! So in hindsight, I'd done the right thing. Yep. Vindication!

"In that case, you should have given me a command."

"But I did give you a command."

"No. Just like you commanded me to capture that Adjutant alive, if you had only commanded me to capture Burks alive, then you needn't have shed your own blood."

I blinked a couple times. I felt like slapping my hand to my forehead. *R-right. That was also an option.* My smug vindication was torn to pieces, flying into the ether. If I had to give a command, shouldn't it have been something like *"Capture Super Sil!"* or *"Knock him out without hurting him!"*...?

Yeah. From the way Klifford handily beat that Adjutant, he could have carried out either of those commands flawlessly. But my train of thought didn't go in that direction at all! I was just obsessed with the idea of snapping Sil out of his trance so Klifford wouldn't perceive him as an enemy...

"My protection means nothing if you harm yourself, Your Highness."

Urk...

"Harm coming to you while I am by your side... It makes me furious. Even if it was by your own hand." His indigo eyes fell on my still-extended left hand. On the white cloth he had wrapped around it. Blood was starting to seep through it. "I couldn't stop you. That makes me terribly furious with myself."

"But...*that* was why I gave that command." So that nobody could hamper my actions—and that included Klifford. That's when I cut my hand, he grabbed my wrist, and I was a little startled.

"It still makes me furious," Klifford snapped quietly.

"Is that...what it means to be an Adjutant?"

For once, Klifford was caught off guard. After a beat, he answered,

"Yes…maybe so." His eyes were cast slightly downward in thought—and from that angle, I caught a glimpse of something on his neck.

My eyes shot wide open. Near the back of his neck, on the lower-left-hand side, the tip of a large gash was showing. I moved before I could even think—my right hand reaching out to Klifford. Naturally, Klifford noticed and turned to look at me. His gash sank behind his collar. He blocked my hand before I could touch it.

"You're wounded."

"It's an old wound… It is unrelated to the fight I just had."

I took a closer look at the vertical slash, and there was indeed no blood. I think. His suit collar hadn't been ripped, and it was still white—that proved it. But still…

"Is that true?"

"If you doubt me, then would you like to see for yourself?" Klifford tilted his head, and the wound appeared again. I ran my fingertip along it. It was sealed… It was a healed wound.

But at a glance, it was crisp, and the scar ran deep—so deep that it almost looked like a fresh wound. The collar on this white uniform was lower set than the collar of his royal bodyguard's uniform. That was why the movements of his head had exposed part of his scar.

"Does it still hurt?"

"No. All that remains is an exaggerated scar."

That's good to hear… I mean, if he'd gotten that gash during the fight just now, my hand cut would be small potatoes…

"Your Highness?"

And then I had an epiphany. "It's because I'm a princess… That's why I'm headstrong." Klifford's eyebrow raised slightly. "You say that my being harmed makes you furious? Well, I feel the same way."

"Is it the same, though?"

"If you got hurt protecting me, I would be very upset. I would be terribly furious, what's more."

"………" Klifford kept staring at me in silence.

"That's why my bodyguard must do more than simply protect me. He must also protect himself from harm—at all times."

"But I haven't been harmed…"

"I know. But you were harmed in the past, weren't you?" As I touched and looked at it, I was sure that his scar told of a very gruesome day. "Klifford. As long as you are in my service, I will not allow you to be hurt any further than this."

Even I thought my demand sounded illogical and crazy. Like, *Where do you get off, bitch?* But that was just the result of me trying to put my epiphany into words. I only felt the way I did—I was only able to keep it together—because Klifford hadn't been hurt.

Even though my bodyguards had changed so frequently, none of them were ever hurt in the line of duty. Before Klifford, I'd never even seen any of them fight an enemy up close before—except for Gray, my first love. And all of that might have just been a lucky coincidence.

"Even a Sovereign hates it when her Adjutant is hurt."

Klifford showed no implications of replying. And after I'd had a good, satisfying rant, I finally calmed down. Well, I was technically calm before, but looking back now, I realize I should have organized my thoughts a little more before I opened my big mouth…

I should've also considered, like, the sequence of events? I mean, *Klifford* was the one who was furious to begin with, and I was just trying to apologize… I broke out in a cold sweat. *Errrm, let's see, maybe I should pull my hand away first? Yeah, let's start with that.*

Just as I was finally about to move my right hand from Klifford's neck, his hand covered it…but only lightly. I could have easily moved my hand away if I wanted to.

"Regarding your command…that I never let myself be harmed…"

Just like the moment I became his Sovereign, Klifford's lips touched the back of my hand, then parted. Fire surged through my veins, and that complicated symbol appeared on my hand. Klifford's Insignia.

It seemed even more vivid than it was when I first saw it two days before. Klifford's eyes widened a little when he saw the Insignia. And then a small smile formed on his lips. It was a mysterious smile.

"Let this Insignia be a testament of my answer."

That was his answer…to my crazy request, right? To the whole "Protect me but make sure you never get hurt, either!" schtick.

His Insignia—the mark glowing on my hand—is a testament?

I parted my lips to say his name—

"Using Sil as bait— Don't you think there was a better way?" Derek's voice boomed loudly through the Sky Chamber, reminding me with a jolt where I was.

I jerked my right hand back to me. The mark on my hand disappeared as I did this. The last time it appeared, it was only for a brief moment. Why had it shone so much longer this time?

And whoa, even though we were standing close to each other and therefore speaking very quietly, Klifford and I just had a pretty damning conversation with words like Adjutant and Sovereign flying to and fro…! Smooth move, Octavia.

I nervously scanned the Sky Chamber. But the battle was won, and we were already in the cleanup phase. The whole Sky Chamber was abuzz with chatter and movement. The soldiers were tying up the traitors. The two Adjutants—one of them unconscious—were being bound with extra care. Our safety was properly ensured. That's my Uncle Dearest!

"Father, I highly doubt Princess Octavia's actions were part of your plan. I'm not sure how you were planning on ensuring Sil's safety had she not taken them."

The voice came from the left of where Klifford and I were standing and Sil was passed out. Uncle Dearest had left his spot near the entrance and was moving freely about the Sky Chamber. He now stood beside the defeated Adjutant. And Derek stood immediately in front of his father, questioning him loudly.

"If it really worries you so, then perhaps you should go over and ensure Mr. Burks's safety before snapping at me?"

"I don't have to go over to him; it's clear he's fine. He's only passed out… I watched it happen."

"Still, if he's your friend, it would seem appropriate for you to run over to him with worry."

"Sorry to disappoint you, but I *am* your son."

Is it just me, or are they at each other's throats?

"Duke Nightfellow! Lord Derek!" I shouted, silencing them both.

I rose to my feet as Derek and Uncle Dearest approached me. Derek was the polar opposite of the esteemed nobleman I'd danced with in the main hall. His clothes were drenched in dark red blood. But since he looked alive and well...I couldn't help but wonder if it was all blood of people he'd attacked and/or killed.

"......Are you unharmed?" I cautiously asked him.

"You needn't worry, Princess. Everything's fine."

That's Uncle Dearest's son for you. The son of Duke Nightfellow wore the smile of nobility. (Sans the blood, of course.)

"It appears *you* are the one who was harmed, Princess Octavia. And Sil—" Derek cut off, a catch in his voice.

I could tell what he was thinking about. It was how inhuman Super Sil had been—and what had led to him snapping out of it.

"Lord Derek, please take care of Lord Sil for me."

Sil showed no signs of waking. I'd wiped my blood from his face, but we couldn't just leave him in the Sky Chamber like this. We needed to let him rest somewhere else. And the only person who I could trust Sil with in that state—in any state, really—was Derek.

Derek sighed and nodded. "Of course, Princess. I'll take care of him."

"Thank you."

Derek propped one of Sil's arms around his shoulder and turned to look at Uncle Dearest. "Father. We'll talk later, but just so you know, I'll be borrowing *your little friend* for a while. I'm sure you have no problem with that. Unless you still *need* him?"

"I don't mind."

By *your little friend*, Derek meant the man who was standing a few paces away from Uncle Dearest at that moment—the redhead.

Duke Nightfellow's little friend in question cried out in protest. "Aw, please, Your Excellency, Lord Derek, both of you, I'm right *here*! Could you please not discuss borrowing me and having your way with me…? Shouldn't I be at least allowed to chat with Princess Octavia first?"

The redhead sounded…shallow. Was this really the same person I'd danced with in the pleasaunce hall?

Derek shot an icy death glare at the redhead. "Why must you be like this…? Just shut up and come with me."

"Oooh, I don't like the sound of that. Lord Derek, you intend to force me to divulge what I may or may not have done."

"Don't be silly. You'll only divulge what you *have* done."

"Okay, fine, I'll tell you what I've done, but once Burksie wakes up, I get to chat him up again."

"Um…… Burksie?"

Burksie?

Derek's scornful muttering and my internal monologue did a little duet. I mean, he called him Burksie. *Burksie!* That redhead… There's more to him than meets the eye!

My brain…is pain. Though not grammatically correct, that was unironically the perfect way of describing the look on Derek's face. With a deep sigh and a grunted "C'mere" at the redheaded man, he rehoisted Sil onto his shoulder. Several soldiers ran over to help him. Now Sil was in good hands.

As I heaved a little sigh of relief, Uncle Dearest's calm voice embraced me. "Your Highness, I'm sure there are things you wish to discuss, but first we must have a physician attend to your wound. You'll need to return to the junior ball at once. Allow me to escort you."

Ordinarily, I'd jump at an invitation from Uncle Dearest like this. But receiving proper treatment would mean leaving the Sky Chamber.

"Please, wait, Duke Night—I mean, Uncle Dearest." It's about time I just call him Uncle Dearest in my mind and out loud! "We can talk here."

"With all due respect… This isn't the sort of place anyone should be in for very long."

"Uncle Dearest, something's been tugging at my mind..." I took a step away from the entrance—and then I froze. The once beautiful Sky Chamber was now a scene of carnage.

I knew we were safe now, but the traces of battle remained as they were. Bodies lay still, the air reeked of blood, and the floor, now red, was littered with weapons. It was the sort of scene where a lady would hesitate to swagger about indifferently as if she was oblivious to the battle that had just unfolded.

N-no, wait a minute, if I just resign my shoes to getting ruined, then hike up the hem of my skirt, then...y-yeah, it'll work out!

"Pardon me."

My vision shifted suddenly. The person who just apologized scooped me off the ground. Klifford's hands rested beneath my back and the backs of my knees.

"Klifford...?"

"Yes, Your Highness? Is there a problem?"

What's the problem? This is a bridal carry!

"I advise against walking in this room. You'll dirty your gown."

R-right. He's doing his job... Well, that just took ten years off my life!

Every girl *dreams* about a handsome man carrying her in his arms! I never experienced it in my past life. And now that I'm a princess, I figured it would happen at least once... Careful what you wish for, Octavia! Now that I was actually experiencing it, the reality of it was just...

Doesn't it, like, take a lot of strength to be the lifter in this scenario? More importantly, my weight...

"I'm not too heavy, I hope?"

"You're not. However, if you would wrap your arms around my neck like last time, that would be more stable."

Like last time? When did I—? Oh! When Klifford and Sil were fighting. "Is it...easier for you to walk that way?"

"Yes."

My mind a whirlpool of conflict, I wrapped my arms around Klifford's neck. He was right—it was more stable this way for me, too. But the fact that I'd done this during the fight without even thinking about it scared me a little.

Klifford glanced around the Sky Chamber. "Where shall I carry you?" he asked, looking down at me.

I turned my gaze toward the farthest recess of the room. Behind the golden throne, where the blue cenotaph was. Rust was standing in front of it. From my vantage point, the blue cenotaph in question was hidden by the throne.

"Your Highness, is that what's been tugging at your mind? Queen Idéalia's cenotaph?" The one who spoke was Uncle Dearest, who was looking into the farthest recess of the Sky Chamber with me. "Well, allow me to accompany you there," Uncle Dearest said softly.

44

With Uncle Dearest leading the way, Klifford carried me through the Sky Chamber. We came close enough to the blue cenotaph to read the letters engraved on it. Rust was right in front of it, his naked longsword dangling at his side.

I'm not sure why, but I felt a horrible sense of wrongness. From what I could see of Rust from my vantage point diagonally behind him, he didn't look heavily wounded. A part of his clothes was stained red, but if you forgot for a moment that there had just been a battle, the splash of red was actually rather beautiful. He was still wearing his silvery-blue mask, too.

It wasn't clear that Rust had had an easy fight, but if his skills with a sword were anything like they were in the source material, it's likely he made good use of them. And yet, even though his mask hid his expression—I sensed something from him. He was staring at the cenotaph as if it had bewitched him. He didn't even notice us approaching... like he had no awareness of his surroundings whatsoever.

When I was about to call out to Rust, he moved. His left hand touched his forehead—the side with the scar. He pressed it hard, shaking his head slightly. It was similar to the motion he had made back in the garden. Was it another episode of phantom pain?

Rust murmured something, balling his dangling right hand into a fist. He raised his longsword, about to—

"Don't!" I yelled.

Rust froze to a halt.

Th-that was close! "What do you think you're doing?" I asked.

Rust turned only his face toward me a little. "I was merely trying to get a better look at this cenotaph, Your Highness…"

He was about to slash his sword through the cenotaph itself—the cenotaph of Queen Idéalia Esfia. The same name that had spilled out of Rust's lips once before.

"And why, pray tell, would you need to desecrate her grave to accomplish that? It would be like killing the dead a second time." I mean, that's quite a violent way to "get a better look" at something! You must respect the dead. I don't care what world you come from; *everybody* knows that!

"Killing the dead a second time?" Rust sneered. "What a fabulous expression. Everybody knows the dead cannot die again." And then he lowered the longsword, threatening the cenotaph no longer. What's more, he set the sword down on the ground and raised his arms upward in a V. A soldier rushed to him, confiscated the sword, and scooted back several paces. Another pair of soldiers stood on either side of the cenotaph, on standby to restrain Rust.

Uncle Dearest and Klifford also stayed where they were, a few paces away from Rust. Meanwhile, the man in question addressed me shamelessly, "Princess Octavia, won't you be a dear and inform Duke Nightfellow that I was your guide? Despite the fact that the son of Duke Nightfellow and I protected you from being taken captive by the intruders, these soldiers seem to think of me as suspect. They're wary of me, even though I've surrendered my weapon."

As he gave his little speech, I noticed that the wrongness I sensed earlier was gone. "Perhaps you deserve it?" Even though Rust claimed he was just trying to get a better look at the cenotaph, it was alarming of him to suddenly raise his weapon—even if we did have the situation under control.

"Harsh words, Princess."

He wanted me to put in a good word for him with Uncle Dearest... That's kind of a tall order. He did safely guide me to the Sky Chamber where Sil was, just like I'd asked. For a short time, we were on the same team. But from our conversation in the garden, I'd gathered he was an anti-royalist. And in the source material, he'd crossed swords with Sirius. So it wasn't like I could give Uncle Dearest glowing reviews of the guy and be like, "*He's totally our ally! You definitely don't need to keep tabs on this guy!*"

Now, if Rust had agreed to be my fake boyfriend as I'd originally intended, that would be a different story—but seeing his face made that plan fly out the window. Not only was Rust the spitting image of that mysterious man, but the sight of him had deeply disturbed my father, too. That was a point I couldn't overlook. Wouldn't it be to my advantage, moving forward, to keep an eye on him?

Still, he did safely guide me here. And a part of me did feel like I owed him my gratitude. Hmmm...

As I sat there, pondering, Uncle Dearest's soft voice reached my ear. "You say you guided Her Highness here. Well, how did you know the way?"

"By chance."

"By *chance*. I suppose you could have heard about the secret passageway through the throne in the first Sky Chamber by *chance*. But what about the rest? The secret passageway that leads here is a tangled labyrinth of tunnels. No, would it be more correct to say the tunnels change their appearance?"

The tunnels...change their appearance?

"Each tunnel has several armed traps. Some of these traps are triggered simply by taking a wrong turn. Walls spring up in the distance, boxing intruders in. Only those who know the right way to walk can make it to the Sky Chamber."

It has that many booby traps?!

"Are you saying you knew all of that by *chance*, as well?" His tone was calm, but I could tell it was checkmate. Uncle Dearest, what a man! That was so badass!

Hey, stop fangirling, Octavia... Use your brain.

Okay. Originally, Rust was tasked by Countess Rosa to seek out the intruders who were after me. And in doing so, he happened to learn of the plot to kidnap Sil—the one the Adjutants were behind.

"In spite of what you may say, my lord, I must insist it *was* by chance."

"So you just happened to know the right order to walk through the tunnels?"

"Yes, Duke Nightfellow. By chance, I happened to overhear how to navigate the tunnels, and I made a mental note of it. And I consider myself extremely lucky to have been able to use this knowledge to serve Her Highness."

Fascinating! The more he talks, the more he smells like bullshit!

To paraphrase, he was really saying *"It wasn't by chance, but do you honestly think I'd tell you the truth? Oh, hell, no!"*—I just knew it! Yeah, I was right the first time. Rust deserved to be suspected! If he really wanted us to trust him, then he'd sure better act trustworthy!

"And were you not satisfied by my service, Your Highness?"

Urk! You're putting me in the hot seat now?

But that was fair. I was unwilling—or rather, *unable*—to give a quippy retort like Uncle Dearest. Because after all, *I* was the one who had asked Rust to be my guide! It was my responsibility to give an explanation.

"Rust—remove your mask and identify yourself to my dear uncle."

Even if it wasn't by chance that Rust had known the way here, I still believed he wasn't in league with the traitors who had captured Sil. That seemed clear from the way the Adjutants were behaving. And in order to get Uncle Dearest to understand that, knowing Rust's true identity was essential! I mean, he was still wearing his mask. If a random outsider saw him now, they'd think he was sketchy

I mean, could *you* trust a masked man? Nay! He must first introduce himself, mask off! Seeing a person's face just makes you feel so much safer! That's just human psychology!

"Your Highness... Did you say that in earnest?" For some reason, Rust questioned my command.

"Yes, I did," I answered quickly.

In comparison, Rust's response was slow. He paused several beats before he answered, "If that is your will..." He lowered his raised hands to remove his mask. The soldiers sprang into action, but Uncle Dearest stopped them with a motion.

He removed the silvery-blue mask, revealing the face that—aside from the scar—was a perfect replica of that mysterious man. I felt my grip tighten around Klifford's neck. This was my third time seeing Rust's bare face. The first time was in the pleasaunce hall. The second was in the garden. And even now, into my third time, I still couldn't remain completely calm.

"As Her Highness commanded, I shall identify myself, Duke Nightfellow," Rust said like a proper nobleman, with an elegant little bow. "My name is Rust Byrne. I am the eldest son of Viscount Byrne, and due to certain circumstances, I am currently in Countess Reddington's employ. Allow me to apologize for the hideous scar on my brow."

And just like me, when Uncle Dearest learned Rust's true identity, his aura changed—

—not even slightly!

Everything about Uncle Dearest's demeanor remained exactly the same. He just stood there, an aura of peacefulness about him, as he stared at Rust's scar in silence.

Is he...processing the news?

"Uncle Dearest?" I was the one who broke the tension in the air. Come on, Uncle Dearest, give us *something* to work with here!

Of course, Uncle Dearest wouldn't ignore me. He smiled at me and said, "Your Highness, do you believe this man is our ally?"

"Of course not!" *Hell, no!* Oopsie. I was going to just give him a plain no, but my personal feelings got in the way.

"That really hurt, Your Highness." Rust chuckled deeply—he was definitely not even slightly hurt.

I want a do-over! With a little cough, I continued, more regally this time, "However, Uncle Dearest, I do not believe he was in league with the traitors who abducted Lord Sil. He fought by my side. It was I who gave him that longsword." I pointed at the longsword the soldiers had confiscated. When I'd glanced at Derek and Rust during the battle, they were cooperating. If Rust had been in league with the Adjutants, the fight likely would have resulted in Derek's capture anyway.

"My apologies for not saying so sooner, but I am glad to see you are unharmed, Rust."

"Likewise, Your Highness…" Rust cut himself off—his amber eyes focused hard on Klifford as he held me in his arms. "You and your bodyguard were both quite heroic, Your Highness. You against Sil Burks—and the bodyguard against the Adjutant."

Unlike me, who had to grasp at straws, Rust seemed well appraised of the battle conditions. But that fact did make this all seem a little strange. It was strange that Rust had been so fixated on Queen Idéalia's cenotaph. Looking back, when Uncle Dearest had arrived, he was focused on the cenotaph then as well.

His behavior was also strange in the garden, when he'd murmured the name of Idéalia. Did Rust know about Idéalia, the queen who was erased from the history books? When he nearly brought his sword crashing down on her cenotaph, was it really so he could *have a closer look* at it? Or was that merely a cover for his real reason—?

"For now, I will hold judgment on this man for later. Will that suffice?" Uncle Dearest's voice snapped me back to reality.

"Yes, Uncle Dearest."

"I trust Your Highness's discernment. However, please permit me to ask him a few questions. I will ask him *only questions pertaining to this incident*. When I'm finished, I will return him to Countess Reddington. Is this acceptable, Your Highness?"

In other words, Uncle Dearest would refrain from asking Rust how he knew the way through the secret passage, but he would still give him a little background check.

"Of course. I have no problems with that."

"Neither do I. As long as *the questions are brief.* And I don't suppose you wish to question me here." Rust stared at Duke Nightfellow, who stared right back. With a shrug, Rust said, "Let me just put my mask back on." And he did so.

"My soldiers will show you the way."

"Aye! Step this way." One of the soldiers on standby gestured to Rust.

As Rust was following the soldiers out of the room, he stopped and turned. "Right, I forgot something very important. I must give Princess Octavia my formal farewell."

A formal farewell? I don't think that's really necessary...

Or so I thought.

"If possible, I wish to receive Your Highness's blessing." His cryptic request hit me like a brick.

My...blessing? Does he mean, like, in the Esfian-way? That thing I did with Alec? A kiss on the cheek to wish someone a safe journey—?

"You wish that...from me? But why?" The utter confusion I felt deep in my heart showed in my voice. The customary blessing only worked if it was between two kindred spirits! Like Alec and me! On reflection, if I gave Rust my parting blessing, I almost think it would have an adverse effect on us... No, it *definitely* would!

And besides, you only do that when someone's leaving on a journey! "Do you mean to say you're leaving on a journey?"

"Depending on how you think about it, leaving your service—moving from one station to another—isn't that a journey of sorts?"

That's quite a reach, my dude! Hmmm... Does he have some sort of plan up his sleeve? Something dangerous, perhaps...as an anti-royalist. But there's no way Rust could outwit Klifford's and Uncle Dearest's sharp eyes!

"I would be honored if Your Highness would accept a little blessing from me as well."

"Do you mean to say I, too, am going on a journey?"

"Yes, you might say your journey is from today to tomorrow."

After a moment's thought, I asked Klifford to set me down. He shot me a questioning look, and I nodded in reply.

I walked over to Rust. *Let's just get this over with!* "Rust Byrne, I give you my blessing." I placed my lips beneath Rust's mask near his right cheek without touching it, then I pulled away. To everyone else, it would look like I had really kissed him—only Rust would know the truth.

Rust's lips raised into a smirk. Then he leaned forward, quite casually toward my left cheek... But whether he wanted to or not, he must have seen the Lieche orchid in my hair. He faltered for a split second. Then his mouth moved close to my left cheek—rather, to my left ear.

"——— ——— ———" And the words he whispered into my ear during the feigned kiss made my eyes open wide. Then he continued louder, "All right, Your Highness. May we both have the best of luck on our journeys."

And it really was good-bye that time—guided by the soldiers, Rust left the Sky Chamber behind him.

Uncle Dearest and I were before the blue cenotaph where Rust had been standing. Klifford was a few feet behind me, and a couple of Uncle Dearest's guards stood at the ready.

"Truly—a disturbing, haunting sight," Uncle Dearest said out of nowhere.

Huh?! I shuddered. *Disturbing? Haunting? Does he mean me?*

"Those were the words he said when he raised his sword—at least, that's what we deciphered after stringing the disjointed words together."

Oh, phew... I thought Uncle Dearest was admitting to hating me all this time! I'd never be able to live that down! I'd just crawl into a hole and die!

After all, I've been referring to my memories between my past life and this one as "shitty haunting memories." The word *haunting* hits a nerve with me. It has super-negative connotations.

"Haunting…" *See? Just voicing it out loud made my chest ache! No, wait a minute. Uncle Dearest wasn't saying that about me! Rust was saying it to the cenotaph… The cenotaph?*

"As I trust your discernment, Your Highness, I will not pursue the matter further… But I don't believe he was swinging his sword at Queen Idéalia's tomb. It seemed more like he was venting his feelings—the cenotaph was merely the spark that lit the fuse."

The spark that lit the fuse… So if Rust really was experiencing phantom pains, then the cause of it was…the cenotaph?

I took another step closer to the blue cenotaph of Queen Idéalia Esfia and hunched over, recalling the words Rust had whispered in my ear during the feigned blessing.

"The dent of the first letter is the number of the sky."

The blessing didn't matter one bit to him. He'd only used it as a diversion to give me that message. But what did it mean? The dent of the first letter? What dent? The number of the sky? I wish I could go back in time and say, *"Not so cryptic, please!"*

It makes me think he was vague on purpose!

But the answer lay on the cenotaph before my very eyes. The first letter—that was the name, carved in the blue stone. And the number of the sky—in honor of the Sky God—was three.

The first letter of the name Idéalia *three times—*

What was I supposed to do?

I touched the letter. *Oh! The whole letter is sinking into the stone…I think. Can I…push it?* I traced the other letters just in case. And the others didn't sink in, despite the fact that they all looked like they had been carved exactly the same way.

Push it three times? Let's try it!

I pushed the letter…and fell silent. I just assumed this would make Rust's message clear! He'd said it so meaningfully that I got my hopes up, but nothing was happening! Was I not supposed to push it three times? Or was this all some elaborate ruse?

Yeah, that has to be it. I mean, why would Rust know about some secret mechanism on the blue cenotaph? Well...then again, since Rust knows so much about Paradise in the Sky, it's still definitely a possibility.

"There's a lid... It appears to be a bit loose," Uncle Dearest said, his voice tense with astonishment.

I rose to my feet and squinted, scanning the cenotaph a few millimeters from the top. Then I saw it—one of the stones toward the top was missing. The cenotaph was a hollow box—a coffin. For a moment, I thought it might contain her remains, but they wouldn't have been placed there.

I reached out with my right hand and touched the coffin lid... Oh! It's made of stone, but it moves smoothly, like it's on wheels. You could slide it to the side with very little effort. As far as mechanisms went, it was rather simple once you knew about it—just like the throne had been.

Once I finished sliding the lid aside, a square-shaped hole remained. It went pretty deep. Something was stuck snugly inside—once I saw it, I reached in with both hands and lifted it out.

I had memories of this. Whenever there was a significant event in Esfia, my father would always wear something of the exact same color and shape.

No... Maybe *this* was it. The golden crown, studded with shining gemstones of all sizes, had been lying dormant inside Idéalia Esfia's tomb.

45

Well. What a crazy thing I just unearthed.

I kind of wonder if the crown back at the castle is a fake, and this is the real one.

It was ridiculous idea, I know! But I got the feeling that my ever-unreliable sixth sense was right on the money this time! And...I actually kinda had some proof I was right.

Okay, okay, okay! I still wasn't 100 percent sure I was right. But there was one part of the crown that would probably help me determine its authenticity.

I gave it another hard looking over just to be sure…and I spotted it.

Let me take you back to a time in this world when I was in peak fujoshi form. I would follow my nose wherever the intoxicating scent of BL carried me. And my fancies carried me to the castle library to excavate new books.

And what I discovered there was a number of drawings of the coronations of the kings through history. Some of the sketches were quite detailed, while some were minimalistic scribbles. Some of them were colored, and others focused solely on the king himself. You could see how drawing styles evolved throughout the ages.

Since cameras didn't exist in this world, if you wanted to immortalize an event, it was all about drawings. Even though that wasn't the intended purpose of those drawings, they were like hidden treasures to me! Oh, I was obsessed. I'd line up the scribbled sketches in chronological order, and I would read the accounts, tasting them with my eyes. Well, I was starved! And if I pretended the drawings were manga, they were really fun to look at! And everything was a novelty, at that!

And thanks to my rabid fujoshi heart (I guess?), I learned that there were two types of crowns in the drawings. Esfian kings all wore the same kind of crown since the dawn of time. But there was one difference: Some crowns had blue amber with an insect inside of it. And some didn't.

When I say "amber," you might envision a sort of honey color. But I'm talking about *amber*—hardened resin. It comes in a variety of colors, including blue. And some of the drawings I found in the castle library told me that not only did some royal crowns contain *blue* amber—they had *insects* inside!

The crown that one of the first kings of Esfia ever wore contained blue amber with an insect in it. But through the ages, the blue gemstone on the left-hand side of the crown lost its insect. And why was that?

As I stared at the art treasures before me, I was faced with a conundrum. I pictured my father, wearing his crown. *His crown has quite a few blue gemstones... But, um, what was it actually like again?*

Seeing the real thing would give me the quickest answer. So I sneaked into the castle depository to have a look! Well, I actually wasn't that badass—the day before the king was to wear his crown at a special event, it was always sort of put on public display for a limited time, so all I had to do was swing by that room to have a look.

For reference, I took a couple drawings from my treasure trove with me: one with the insect-filled amber and one without. Then all I had to do was use my Princess Privilege to get rid of the other people around.

But I didn't have to get rid of anyone. The only person there was Alec, who'd happened to come in earlier to have a look at the crown. And having Alec there wasn't a problem. In fact, I welcomed his company!

So with my drawings in hand, and with a keen eye, I opened my investigation. Father's crown—it did have the blue amber. But there wasn't a trace of an insect. Both of my drawings showed each crown's uniqueness in great detail. And the only difference between the drawing and the real thing was the insect in the amber.

Alec looked back and forth between the drawing and the actual crown. "Sister... This crown... Is it not the real one?" Alec asked in confusion. The clever boy had picked up on the difference.

Was this precious heirloom that had been handed down through the generations swapped out a long time ago? This gave birth to a doubt in my mind. It was still just a doubt—remember that for later.

As long as there wasn't another crown somewhere that had blue amber *with* an insect in it, then this crown was the one and only! The real deal! At least that's what I decided to believe.

I turned to Alec and said solemnly, "Let's pretend we didn't see this."

Alec's emerald-green eyes widened momentarily. Then he smiled like an angel and nodded. "All right, Sister..."

"Well, hello there, you two." Uncle Dearest had entered then, suspicious of all the displaced people. Ordinarily, I would be overjoyed to see him, but I was rather nervous to see him then. When he asked me about the drawings in my hand, I showed him just one of the drawings as if it was nothing important—my heart quietly racing all the while.

Uncle Dearest asked no further questions and returned the drawing to me. Then Alec and I beat a hasty retreat.

Now. Back to the present—

The crown was a rather perfect weight to be held in both hands. It was adorned with blue amber…blue amber with an insect inside!

Curiosity killed the cat.

Aaaggghhh. I got the problematic kind of crown. M-maybe I could put it back and pretend I didn't see it…

While I was busy having a quiet freak-out, a shadow loomed over the crown. It was Uncle Dearest. He was running his eyes over the crown, trying to appraise it. I looked up at him in distress.

Hey. Uncle Dearest. What shall I do with this thing? Any thoughts? Authenticity aside, I don't think it's good that it looks way too similar to the crown we keep at the castle! Especially when you consider where we found it…

Should we just sweep it under the rug? Or maybe Uncle Dearest should just put it on and give us the Good Ending of his character route! I could wear the other crown!

While I was busy letting my mind wander where it shouldn't, Uncle Dearest muttered, "That it would be inside Queen Idéalia's cenotaph…" He immediately followed it with a burst of escaped laughter.

I have no idea what's so funny, Uncle Dearest! I stared up at him, my eyes fluttering with confusion.

He apologized through his chuckles, then he explained, "It was startling to find it in a place like this."

Whoa, hold up, Uncle Dearest… It was startling to find the crown "in a place like this"? Not, it was startling "to find this crown" at all?

"His Majesty will be pleased. He has been searching for the true crown for quite some time."

My father...has been searching...for the true crown? Mmmrrrggg?

"Uncle Dearest. The crown at the castle..."

"You want to know what it is? Well, didn't you and Prince Alexis once visit the castle depository to check its authenticity? You had two drawings with you."

He saw right through me! Oh, Uncle Dearest, what sharp eyes you have! But from the way he was speaking just now...

I looked at the crown in my hands. "The crown back at the castle is a fake. Does anybody else besides you know that?"

If he was like "*Yup, everybody knew all along! It's common knowledge among the royalty and upper nobility!*" that would be a huge blow to my ego. I mean, what would that make me? As the one person who didn't know...

Uncle Dearest smirked sympathetically and shook his head. "No, Princess. As far as the public knows, the crown His Majesty wears is genuine. There's a handful of us, though, who have heard stories about King Eus—that he lost the crown before his enthronement and quickly had a replica made. And that the replica is the crown we use today."

Well, what do you know! That was an account that never showed up in any of the texts on King Eus I'd pored over. That was surprising, since there were plenty of far-fetched episodes in the collection. I guess that meant somebody left the crown out on purpose.

"However, those of us who have heard the rumor never speak of it. Nobody believed it was true, either."

"Must his crown...stay hidden forever?"

King Eus lost the crown and replaced it with a replica—the very crown we still use today. The insect-filled blue amber was the one part of the crown that could not be replicated. Yeah, that's a scandal for the ages.

If this had been recorded in our historical texts, that would be another matter entirely. But the crown in the castle was universally accepted as the true crown passed down through the royal family since Esfia's first king. Anyone who claimed it was a fake would be accused of treason.

"You are the first person I've discussed this with, Your Highness. And likewise, haven't you kept quiet about this second crown all these years as well?"

"Well, yes. I didn't have any proof. Talking about it would have only caused needless disturbance."

Let sleeping crowns lie, I say.

I mean, it's the crown—the frickin' *crown*! It's like, the royal family's greatest treasure. It didn't matter how deeply the seed of doubt had taken root inside of me. Drawings were pretty weak evidence that it was fake. I also figured there was probably some reason behind the whole thing...

"Indeed. It is quite difficult for us to know with certainty what happened in the past. Sometimes, what we thought existed didn't exist. Other times, what we thought didn't exist actually did. Either case is possible. Besides, human beings are liars. We lie intentionally. We lie unintentionally. And the latter is the one that's more difficult to deal with. Without proof, it was impossible to prove that the crown is a fake."

It *was* impossible. He used the past tense on purpose. Because now I had the proof in my hands.

"Unless somebody found the true crown?"

"Indeed, Your Highness." He nodded. "Now that you have the true crown, that changes everything. To irreverent bastards, that crown is the ideal weapon to denounce the royal family. In actual fact, many people throughout history have searched for King Eus's lost crown— each having their own expectations."

Well, yeah, my father searched for it, too. Makes sense, seeing as how he's the king.

But wait a minute. King Eus...*lost* the crown? As in, by mistake? I looked back and forth between the blue cenotaph and the crown.

Considering the mechanism in the cenotaph…it had to be intentional, right? King Eus, of his own volition, buried the crown along with Queen Idéalia—that's the more correct way of putting it.

Human beings are liars… The words Uncle Dearest spoke only a minute ago reentered my mind. This was a lie King Eus told intentionally. I had the feeling he had all of this in mind.

"Paradise in the Sky was thought to be one of the possible locations for the lost crown due to King Eus's two commands: '*The throne room must remain untouched,*' and '*Paradise in the Sky cannot be returned to the royal family.*' However, nobody thought to look inside the grave of his sister—the queen he killed."

We had tombs in my past life, too—like the pyramids in Egypt or the *kofun* in Japan. And we had our fair share of tomb raiders, too. Just getting here was a big enough ordeal already—most people didn't even know Queen Idéalia had existed…

Oh, right. It's not just the crown that Uncle Dearest was surprised by. It was Queen Idéalia's cenotaph—and Idéalia herself. The queen who was killed by her little brother—the queen purged from history.

"Uncle Dearest, I see you aren't surprised by Queen Idéalia's existence. Or her cenotaph."

"Indeed, no. I knew about her, though in rumor only."

"Though you never spoke about it publicly?"

"Indeed." He nodded with a little smirk. Then he continued quietly, "The fact that the crown was hidden in her tomb… That might be an indication of King Eus's intentions."

Why did King Eus hide the crown in his sister's cenotaph? He did hide it—that much was true. Queen Idéalia was erased from history, but he left a record of her here. In the Sky Chamber—a place where nobody was to enter—and in a secret compartment, besides. He left a record of her not as a mere royal, but as a queen, with her proper name: *Idéalia Esfia.*

"An indication of his intentions…"

"*I am not the king. My sister is the rightful monarch.*" Uncle Dearest took a breath and continued. "But the opposite is just as possible. King Eus feared his sister, the one he killed with his own hands. So he built this cenotaph and the crown replica in order to quell his fears."

I shook my head. "I don't think that's true." What I sensed in this Sky Chamber was a deep reverence and love for the dead. The cenotaph was formal, too, which only made everything more confusing.

"Uncle Dearest... Why do you think King Eus killed his sister? Do you think just maybe...he had no other choice?"

"Given the mental state of the slain Idćalia Esfia, that is within the realm of possibility. What's written in the history books as Eus's accomplishments as king include some of the tasks she accomplished. From that, we can glean that she was a queen who loved her kingdom and her subjects with all her heart. Perhaps *that* was why."

"Because she was the queen?"

"Yes, a queen who lived for her kingdom. Consequently, when nothing could be done to save her, perhaps that was the best way for her to meet her end."

"*That way* being: death by the hand of King Eus?"

"He who slays the evil queen is not a villain but a hero. A hero worthy of being the next king. She died so that she could surrender the kingdom to her brother."

"Was she really an evil queen?"

"If a kingdom is in danger, its people will perceive their ruler as evil."

When she ascended the throne, Esfia fell into chaos. That part wasn't in the source material—that mysterious man might have had a hand in it. If I research King Eus...maybe I can learn a lot more. Maybe, look at Eus from different perspectives. Like, from Khangena's point of view.

"Your Highness, I don't think you should trouble yourself with history. It's nothing that can be changed."

"Then let me ask you this, Uncle Dearest: Can the future be changed?"

"It's certainly easier than changing the past." He nodded firmly.

"Exactly." In spite of myself, I smiled. The future hasn't been determined yet. It can be changed… And I *will* change it.

"You have already changed one aspect of the future, Your Highness. This crown."

I looked down at the crown in my hands… This old thing?

"Perhaps the future ruler of Esfia will don that crown. Its discovery is truly a joyful thing."

He was right. I'd overlooked a necessary condition. Since I found the real crown, giving it to my father would be the right thing to do. But if I *must* give it to him—

"Uncle Dearest… May I make a request regarding this crown?"

"If it's something of which I am capable, I would be honored."

That's my Uncle Dearest! Those words are like music to my ears! I thrust the crown just inches from his face. And with a look of bewilderment, he took the crown.

"I want you to have it and say that you found it."

"You want me…to give it to His Majesty?"

"I think that would be best." I nodded approvingly. This would definitely give Uncle Dearest's standing with my father a big boost! It *kinda* seemed like they never really got along. Like Father wanted to keep him at a distance. Like, a thorn in his side?

Now, I can't deny that my Uncle Dearest bias might be making me see the man through rose-colored glasses. House Nightfellow has always had a good relationship with the royal family, and I can't say my father exactly gave Uncle Dearest the cold shoulder, but if anyone should give my father this crown, it was him.

So I decided we should go ahead and say he found it, too! Though technically, Rust deserved the credit… Given what he'd whispered in my ear, it was highly likely he knew about the crown. But he didn't work the mechanism himself. What *was* going through his head? Hmmm…

"Respectfully, I shall give His Majesty this crown," Uncle Dearest answered.

My eyes sparkled. "Good!"

"However, I wish to tell him that you gave it to me."

Dang, he's a stickler... But that makes my heart flutter! "I under-stand, Uncle Dearest."

With that, he called over one of his soldiers. The soldier ran off for a bit, then returned with a cloth. He spread the cloth wide with both hands, then Uncle Dearest set the crown atop it. Then with a bow, the soldier left.

Good. Uncle Dearest is going to give the crown to my father. Now that that's settled—

"Uncle Dearest, might we also discuss the circumstances of Lord Sil's abduction as well?"

While I've got him here, let's get him to reveal all!

46

Uncle Dearest said he wouldn't mind answering my questions. So I asked, and he answered politely and in detail.

I finally learned everything about the mass capture of the two groups of traitors who had intruded on the junior ball. But what sur-prised me most of all was what had happened with Sil. Apparently, Uncle Dearest had a hand in Sil slipping out of the junior ball and winding up in the Sky Chamber!

Oh, not that Uncle Dearest was in league with the traitors or any-thing. He had gotten wind of the group of traitors with the Adjutants and that they were targeting Sil. So he had gotten Sil himself to coop-erate with his scheme to catch them—which resulted in him going to the group of traitors as bait.

Now it finally made sense why Derek had been so angry with his father. When Uncle Dearest had dashed into the Sky Chamber like a hero, his hand in Sil's capture probably became clear to Derek.

"Your Highness, won't you rebuke me like my good-for-nothing son did?"

"Was this plan…something that Lord Sil agreed to of his own voli-tion?" If that was the case, I couldn't complain. Sil knew the danger he was putting himself in. That's just how desperate he was to meet his birth parents…to find out who he really was. Uncle Dearest told me he didn't know the answer to that either—it was the traitors who had slipped Sil the tip that his birth parents would be at the junior ball. So there was no telling if it was a solid lead…

Now, on to the matter of the Adjutant and Sil… How had Sil turned into Super Sil? Did the Adjutant do something to him?

"Are you about to interrogate them now?" I asked.

Both Adjutants were now apprehended. The younger Adjutant—the one who was still conscious—was undergoing a body check by the Nightfellow soldiers. They'd removed his hood, too. The man's eyes, blue as the crystals that adorned the walls of this room, pierced me with the intensity of a knife. I almost literally jumped in the air.

I snapped my fluffy black wreven feather fan open, shielding myself from the Adjutant's penetrating gaze. That's right! A little while after Uncle Dearest started explaining everything that had happened, Blackfeather returned safely to me! One of the soldiers had picked it up off the ground, but since Uncle Dearest and I were busy talking, he had handed it to Klifford. Klifford then waited for a pause in the con-versation to hand it to me.

"Yes. Luckily, most of the intruders were only wounded, so we'll be able to take them alive. After we transfer them to the royal castle, with His Majesty's permission, we intend to conduct a thorough investigation."

What was that young Adjutant's name again? Emilio, I think? And there was the girl Uncle Dearest had brought into the room who was his Sovereign. I wonder where she is…

"Where's Lady Turchen? She seemed completely oblivious to the plot."

"We're keeping her for insurance. Her Adjutant was one of our per-sons of interest. However, we were unable to determine whether he was in league with the traitors, so from his actions tonight, we were able to determine where he stood. If you want to gain control of an Adjutant with a Sovereign, capture the Sovereign—that's standard procedure. Please do not worry yourself over Lady Turchen. At present, not a hair on her head has been harmed."

"At the very least...the Adjutant didn't seem to be targeting Lord Sil."

"Didn't he turn his blade on you, Your Highness?"

Urk...

"Our investigation may yield some details regarding that. Would you mind giving me your testimony on the events of this evening?"

I felt torn for a minute. I was certainly willing to tell Uncle Dearest anything... But how much should I reveal about Sil? Maybe I should keep my mouth shut about Super Sil?

An answer hit me immediately— *It's futile, Octavia!*

Even from behind my fan, I could feel Emilio's harsh gaze boring into me. And that made me realize that the Adjutants and all the traitors here would tell everything like they saw it! Meaning, if I gave a false testimony, it would bite me in the ass!

I closed Blackfeather and opened my mouth and told him everything. Everything from coming under attack in the garden to Rust guiding me, to meeting up with Derek, to arriving at the Sky Chamber. Then I described the series of events that happened in the Sky Chamber.

"Thank you... That information will be quite useful."

"But I'm afraid I might have interfered with your plan." That's why a part of me still felt sore that I was not consulted beforehand. Though I suppose it might have been unavoidable—his plan involved deceiving his enemies, starting with his allies.

"Interfere? You did nothing of the sort. Though the way you behave never ceases to surprise me, Your Highness."

"Was I...behaving too brashly?"

"I didn't foresee that you would act on your own to find Mr. Burks. Ever since you were a little girl...you always did prefer to take action rather than talk." He smiled his eyes fondly at me.

"Was I like that?" *I had to feign ignorance! That's my dark past you're talking about, Uncle Dearest...*

When I ended my life as Maki and was reborn only a few hours later as Octavia, the Esfian language was totally foreign to me. It took quite a bit of time before I felt confident enough to speak it... I could've just settled on making mistakes as I learned...but the way I made mistakes was pretty unnatural!

So until I was confident enough to speak the Esfian language with grace, I was a princess of very few words. I favored action over talk— well, I had to! If I was shaky on the grammar, I couldn't talk in Esfian! For a time, I survived just off of *yes* and *no*... And since I also had a hard time understanding people, there was a lot of "Could you please slow down?" and "One more time, please?"

"Yes, I remember you well at that age, Your Highness."

Grr! Uncle Dearest, your smile is as bright as the sun!

"It seems you've given up on those mystical incantations, though."

"Well... I was a child. I was just playing pretend."

I studied the Esfian language like I would have studied any other foreign language. I thought in Japanese, because I was scared that I might lose it otherwise—though at the start, this was just because I didn't understand enough Esfian to think in it. In other words, it was inevitable that Japanese words would pop out of my mouth whenever I felt insecure about my Esfian. *Those* were the "mystical incantations" Uncle Dearest was talking about.

The mystical incantations were actually Japanese all along! Even the pinkie-promise song Alec and I sang in Esfian before he departed on his mission—originally, the lyrics were *"Yubikiri Genman"* as they were in Japanese.

Yup! The first time I taught the song to wide-eyed little Alec, it was the Japanese version! And he memorized the words after just one listen, the little genius. It's hard enough to memorize something when its words have meaning—memorizing a short string of random syllables was fiercely difficult! That was one of the occasions on which I caught a glimpse of my baby brother's special gift...

"I'll have you know: I enjoyed listening to your little incantations."

"Uncle Dearest..." *What kindness! What tact! Ah, it touches my heart!*

That being said, Japanese words seldom escaped my mouth anymore in my daily life. I can wield the Esfian language freely now, you see! Never underestimate the power of perseverance! When faced with necessity, you, too, can master a foreign language and be bilingual!

If only I could have applied such perseverance to my English classes in my past life! Well......not sure that would've helped. In Japan, you can get by just fine only knowing Japanese. There's absolutely no necessity for being bilingual at all...

Still, even though I do all my talking in Esfian, I still do most of my thinking in Japanese. I also write my diary in Japanese! It's pretty handy, too. I mean, no matter what I write, I'm the only one who can understand it! It's all in code! Even if somebody ripped out all the pages and posted them all over town, my privacy wouldn't be violated! I think I'll write about what happened today when I get home to the castle. So much happened I'll need to jot down some notes...

"You've gone through countless bodyguards since then, too, Your Highness...," Uncle Dearest said, pausing from his fond reminiscence to steal a glance at Klifford. "I imagine you must deeply trust your current bodyguard. To think that he was able to beat that Adjutant in combat as if he were a spindly rag doll."

Even though the compliment was about Klifford, hearing it from Uncle Dearest filled me with pride. "I am proud to call him my bodyguard."

"Your bodyguard was so powerful—almost made me wonder if he, too, was an Adjutant."

My soul jumped out of my body. *Uncle Dearest. You're a sly one. Did he overhear my conversation with Klifford? No... He wouldn't have phrased it that way if that were the case.*

"I think strong gentlemen who *aren't* Adjutants do indeed exist, Uncle Dearest."

"Indeed. Like the Emissary of Ongarne, for one."

My breath caught in my throat. Ongarne. In the Saza faith, that was their word for Hell. It was also a key word in the Turchen Arc. But I've never heard the phrase "Emissary of Ongarne" before. I've never heard it applied to a person.

My curiosity was whetted. "Uncle Dearest, I would love to know more about this Emissary of Ongarne." Pretty please, Uncle Dearest!

"If my feeble knowledge suffices, Your Highness." He released his fixated gaze from Klifford and smiled back at me.

Awww, I love ya, Uncle Dearest!

"The Emissary of Ongarne is a title a certain man came to be known by during the war with the Saza Church. At the start of the war, Esfia was not at an advantage. But then this man of inhuman strength appeared and assassinated Nathaniel, the rebel who led the Saza Church's forces. However, this man also caused casualties to Esfia's side. Because of this, both sides feared him. From the ruthless way he fought, he came to be known as the Emissary of Hell—in other words, the Emissary of Ongarne. It's believed that the elite soldiers of faith were the ones who named him."

In the war with the Saza Church... A man with inhuman strength...

Well, I was left in the dark about that war... Rather, I, *the princess*, was left in the dark. My father had instructed me to go about my life as usual. Instead, my duties as princess were shifted to *after* the war. At the end-of-war celebration to welcome home the soldiers, I flashed my biggest smiles and offered my condolences to the peasants who'd lost loved ones.

"In that case, Uncle Dearest, isn't it likely that this Emissary of Ongarne is an Adjutant?"

He shook his head no. "That's highly unlikely."

"Why?"

"Because, Your Highness, the Emissary of Ongarne committed acts that an Adjutant would never commit."

"Such as...what?"

"The Emissary of Ongarne assassinated Nathaniel. However—according to what is known about them—no Adjutant should have been capable of killing Nathaniel. Without express permission, an Adjutant cannot defy a Sovereign. And Nathaniel... He belonged to that bloodline."

I racked my brain, digging up everything I'd ever learned about the Saza Church. *Let's see... Okay, I've got something!*

Long ago, when there was an epidemic in Esfia, the chants of a person named Saza brought salvation to the suffering and the dead. Saza amassed quite a number of believers overnight, but as the epidemic came to an end, their numbers dwindled. They've been a small group ever since.

Their sudden revival happened during King Eus's reign—when the Saza Church's leader was chosen hereditarily...

"Was there a reason they adopted that system?"

Uncle Dearest shook his head slightly. "That is beyond my comprehension."

"Oh my... So there are things even you do not understand."

"Princess, I do believe you overestimate my abilities."

"But you are so knowledgeable! So much that I almost wonder if *you* are an Adjutant."

A brief silence fell between us. "Well...for personal reasons, I haven't ever told you this, but actually, I am an Adjutant."

My jaw dropped. Words failed me.

"Pity that was a joke," he added with a playful grin.

"Uncle Dearest!" *That was just too mischievous! I actually believed you!*

He was laughing jovially. "As the head of House Nightfellow, it is only natural that I would know a thing or two about Adjutants—that is all."

Right. Derek did say something about House Nightfellow being a sort of information hub.

"That is why I theorized that this Emissary of Ongarne is merely a man of innate abilities. I never considered that he might be an Adjutant."

"Yes... I suppose you wouldn't." *My declaration was born of ignorance!*

"However, the idea that the Emissary of Ongarne is an Adjutant is most intriguing. It is possible—if there was an Adjutant who could make *possible* what was once *impossible*." He smiled angelically this time.

And I smiled back at him like a cherub—or I tried to, at least. I felt a big yawn coming on, so I snapped Blackfeather open in front of my mouth. I couldn't deceive Uncle Dearest, though.

"You seem tired. Sorry I kept you so late."

"Oh, I am fine, Uncle Dearest." It was my decision to stay behind anyway. I was just feeling a little tired...at an important moment like this, of course! Argh, why? And I had that epic nap in the carriage ride over here, too.

"No, Princess. You should leave this place and go to bed," he prompted me firmly.

Soldiers were bustling about in the Sky Chamber. I guess my presence here would only make them uncomfortable...

I'd better do as Uncle Dearest says. Oh! But first... "Um, Uncle Dearest? About the conversation we just had..."

I was pretty sure he hadn't figured out that Klifford was an Adjutant... At least, I hoped he hadn't. But some of his soldiers might have overheard something, and I just told Uncle Dearest plenty of things I didn't want made public—and yes, I realize I'm noticing this after the fact! Uncle Dearest just puts me at ease, and I couldn't help myself!

"Aside from your bodyguard, yourself, and all the traitors, everyone here is my subordinate. None of them will speak of what they saw or heard in this room. They know what will happen to them if they speak indiscriminately. Unless you *want* to make an announcement to my subordinates..."

I quickly shook my head no. *I'm keeping my mouth shut!*

I started to walk out of the room—but I turned back to look at the cenotaph. The beautiful blue cenotaph.

"Your Highness?"

"Uncle Dearest... I need a moment." On a whim, my uninjured right hand touched my hair. I removed the hair decoration made of two Lieche orchids. When Rust saw these flowers in my hair, he had called me Idéalia. And in a similar fashion, Sil had called me Your Majesty. Maybe the two incidents weren't related. Perhaps it was meaningless.

Everything might just be in my imagination.

But maybe...maybe Queen Idéalia loved to wear real flowers in her hair. And maybe Lieche orchids in particular were her favorite bloom. I set the Lieche orchids on her cenotaph as an offering. Even if my theory was wrong, I wanted to give the flowers to her.

"I'm ready to go now, Uncle Dearest."

When Uncle Dearest ran into the Sky Chamber with his soldiers... Even if the redhead had run ahead to inform him, and even if he'd had another contact, considering the distance we had to walk after operating the mechanism in the throne, Uncle Dearest and his men had arrived too early for any of this to make sense.

So how did it work, you may ask? Here's the answer: Uncle Dearest and his men used a bypath!

"Anyone who knows the proper pathway to take *wouldn't* know about this bypath. It was useless to them. Long ago, somebody decided it would be a good idea to build a new entrance. They drilled a hole through the mountain that connected to the passageway. It was an ambitious project. And I imagine a lot of suffering went along with it."

"Truly. If you went down the wrong path, not only would you become lost, wouldn't the mechanism keep you trapped inside the tunnel as well?" I pondered.

"Yes. But we have their suffering to thank for our swift and easy way into the Sky Chamber."

We were walking through the very tunnel in question. Uncle Dearest and a few of his soldiers, torches in hand, were with us. This tunnel took a lot less time to traverse than the technically correct path that Rust had taken us on. So when Uncle Dearest told me about this tunnel, I decided to take it.

But it was just a tunnel. It wasn't paved or outfitted. This tunnel had a very strong *Road? I'll make my own road, thanks!* vibe to it. There was a magnificent number of rocks scattered everywhere about the ground.

And the damp ground...was amazing at making you slip! I almost fell down many times. Klifford caught me each time, until I finally gave up and had him carry me. It was Carry Me Over the Threshold of our Honeymoon Suite, Part II. No wait, Part III if you include the part where he carried me from the cenotaph to the Sky Chamber's exit...

With my arms wrapped around Klifford's neck, I felt extremely at peace. In spite of that—or maybe...*because* of that?—just like back in the carriage, I kind of didn't feel even slightly sleepy anymore!

My conversation with Uncle Dearest had died down. The only sound I heard was our footsteps echoing in the tunnel. The desire to sleep only grew stronger. Maybe my relief over the ordeal finally being over was the prevailing force. I didn't make any progress in finding a (fake) boyfriend. But so many other things had happened at the junior ball—and I'd already had enough excitement for the day.

Urrrgh. It's no use...

"Your Highness?"

As I nuzzled my face against Klifford's chest and closed my eyes, I was on a collision course with sleep. My body gently rocked in his arms. His chest was warm against my face. I could hear his heart beating. I felt so safe. I was in the perfect place to fall asleep.

But before that happened—I remembered.

In a half-dream state, not quite fully asleep, my lips moved, calling a name. "Klifford..."

I have to tell him.

Listen, Klifford...

"I'm sorry...I worried you."

I had to make sure I apologized for that.

"I see..." I thought I heard a smile in his voice. "Sleep well, Princess."

I will...

I know I won't have that nightmare tonight.

The World Through the Emissary of Ongarne's Eyes: 5

"Did she fall asleep?"

Klifford turned around. Leif Nightfellow was watching Princess Octavia as she breathed softly in her sleep. His charcoal-gray eyes crinkled into a soft smile. But his smile only lasted a few seconds. He looked up and made a proposal to Klifford.

"Sir Knight, might we carry Her Highness?"

His soldiers were standing at the ready, waiting to carry out the order.

Klifford ruminated on his proposal. *Entrust Octavia to him?*

He shook his head. "No, I'll carry her."

Even if it made fighting more cumbersome for him, Klifford could not entrust Octavia to anybody else—he didn't *want* to. Did this feeling come from his Adjutant side? Surely it did, considering how his Insignia had shone even stronger back in the Sky Chamber.

"If, theoretically, we were to turn our swords on you, you wouldn't be able to put up a fight. Is your answer still no?" the duke asked again, as if to test him.

"Do you have such aspirations, my lord?"

Klifford knew that he didn't. He could sense if anyone intended to fight. It was a matter of habit. Be it murderous intent or pure animosity, the act of hiding such intentions always caused emotional turbulence. Every breath, every movement Duke Nightfellow's eyes made refuted any claim that he intended to fight Klifford.

"Of course I don't. I was speaking theoretically. I don't wish to start a fight I cannot win."

".........." Klifford did not respond.

"But if everything I read up on Klifford Alderton is true, you make the choice that is most advantageous in all things. Though I doubt a man who makes his living as a fighter would consider having both his hands tied as an advantage."

The duke was not wrong. When he served his former Sovereign, he might have handed Octavia off, considering her a burden. His top priority was to always be ready for a fight.

"But if I win, the problem is moot."

The charcoal-gray eyes searched Klifford. "I suppose Her Highness wouldn't have let a man with less confidence serve her," he murmured, returning his gaze to Octavia.

"Mm..." Octavia moaned softly, squirming in Klifford's arms. She nuzzled her cheek against Klifford's chest, seeking warmth or comfort. Peace filled her face.

Klifford was aware of the relief he felt. That his Sovereign was not trapped in a nightmare as she had been back in the carriage. Just as a smirk formed on his lips, boisterous laughter erupted around him, betraying the dark cave's dreary atmosphere.

"Personally, I would never be able to sleep at ease in your presence... though the opposite seems to be true of Her Highness. Are you two similar in that way?"

"I do not understand your meaning... I would never harm Her Highness." He shifted her position in his arms carefully, so as not to disturb her slumber. Her grip on his neck loosened, her bandaged left hand falling into view. The white cloth was stained faintly with blood.

The sight of it made him feel furious all over again.

"But Her Highness harmed herself," the duke said, gesturing to his soldiers with his chin. One of the soldiers nodded and handed him a torch. Then the soldiers knowingly put some distance between them and their master, disappearing into the darkness ahead.

Sending his soldiers ahead was a daring move. The duke held his torch high and walked slowly as he spoke. "Did you perhaps overlook that Princess Octavia was about to harm herself under your very nose, Sir Knight? Naturally, she came to your defense—said she had commanded you to let her do it. But as her vassal, I cannot help but worry. If she gives you such a command in the future, will you obey her?"

To an Adjutant, a Sovereign's command is absolute. It transcends ethics, emotion, and will. When Octavia grabbed the dagger and held it to her hand, Klifford understood his Sovereign's intentions. He knew that she had preemptively commanded him not to stop her.

Knowing this, he decided to obey. However...

Klifford had gripped his Sovereign's wrist without meaning to. He remembered the startled look in Octavia's eyes. An emotion consumed him: rage. The instant he saw the red blood spill from Octavia's palm, he could no longer contain it.

He was furious that Octavia had wounded herself so callously...and furious with himself for not stopping her. Had he done so *because* he was her Adjutant? But his feelings contradicted her command.

"Next time...I will not let it happen."

"Do you mean to say that even if she commands it, even if her self-harm is merely a test, that you will not let her spill a single drop of blood?"

"Yes." Klifford nodded firmly. *As long as I am by Octavia's side...*

"Good. If you're acting on your personal feelings, I don't like that—but it's Princess Octavia's choice to make. It is my sincere wish that you can become someone Princess Octavia can let herself be vulnerable around."

An image of Octavia's tearstained face entered Klifford's mind. Her command to hide her.

"She never shows weakness—not in earnest. Sadly, I wasn't good enough for Her Highness—she sees through my true nature." A sarcastic smile flashed on the duke's face for a moment. He looked back at Klifford and continued speaking. "Well, this is all irrelevant. I don't care who you really are—I just wanted to hear you say it would never happen again. Though, of course there are a few more questions I'd love to ask you."

"...No Adjutant should have been capable of killing Nathaniel."
"It is possible—if there was an Adjutant who could make possible *what was once* impossible.*"*

He was reminded of the words the duke had told Octavia back in the Sky Chamber.

"Like, for example, why do you think Mr. Burks was a target of the Adjutants?"

"Please ask the Adjutants who targeted him." The icy words flew out of him, contrasting the warmth from Octavia that he felt in his arms.

Why was Burks a target? That was obvious. It had to do with Sil Burks's background—his blood. And the memories engraved in him, inherited from the Adjutants, were turning the wheels in the direction of ostracization. For an Adjutant held captive by the past, the movements were powerful.

But the captured Adjutants would surely not talk.

"Then let me ask you this: If you were an Adjutant, would Mr. Burks be your target?"

"If I were an Adjutant—*I* would be the target." Klifford's vague answer offered one side of the truth. If his identity was exposed, both he and Burks would become the Adjutants' targets. As abominations who must be exterminated. But this would never come to light—*never*. Thus, neither would he ever become their target.

For when the child of taboo was born of his mother screaming in anguish, it was announced as a stillbirth.

"*You* would be the target, eh? I'll keep that in mind."

"If I may, Duke Nightfellow—I would also like to ask you a question."

The duke turned back to look at him as he walked. "Oh? Do you, Sir Knight?"

"Are you an Adjutant?"

"Hmm. An unexpected question. Did you take my little joke to Princess Octavia seriously?"

"It did not seem like a joke to me."

He sensed it back at the Sky Chamber. At the very least, Leif Nightfellow could hold his own in a fight against an Adjutant—that was just how skilled he was. It didn't matter how many soldiers he had or how prepared they were. His victory against an Adjutant was not guaranteed. If Octavia hadn't involved herself, the duke would have stormed the Sky Chamber with only himself and his small army. He neutralized the immature Adjutant by taking his Sovereign hostage, but what about the other Adjutant? Could he have avoided fighting him as well?

The answer was no.

In that scenario, the chances were high that a sword fight would have ensued—and it would have been Duke Nightfellow himself who won the day. And not easily, either. But Klifford reasoned that the duke would have indeed been able to capture the Adjutant. No matter which way the chips fell, his plan to use Burks as a decoy would have succeeded.

"Both Her Highness and you seem to overestimate my abilities. Though I am flattered, truly."

Adjutants did not possess any sort of unique traits that were obvious on sight. The most obvious trait was their strength, of course—which was exactly what made the duke suspect. If he wasn't an Adjutant, then he truly would be a man of godlike skill.

Or perhaps he had once studied under an Adjutant.

"Well, let me say this much: Even if you hadn't arrived, I did have a means of overpowering the Adjutant," the duke murmured, his soft gaze on the sleeping princess. "I would have won, one way or another.

However…" He paused. "If you hadn't arrived, it is unknown whether Mr. Burks would have remained unharmed. Moreover, I would not have been able to discover the crown on my own."

The crown—

"And what a surprise it was when the princess insisted that *I* be the one to present it to His Majesty. It troubles me, actually." From his words, the duke did not sound amused, but there was a mirthful grin on his face.

Octavia had tasked Leif Nightfellow—who had, up to this point, been at neutral standing in the government—with the honor of presenting King Enoch with the true crown hidden in the queen's tomb. Octavia might have requested this of Duke Nightfellow because she had aspirations for the throne. So that in his moment in the sun, she would be standing in line with him.

No… If the duke presented the crown to the king in place of Octavia—its true discoverer—that respectful act alone would make others associate Octavia with queenliness.

The cave's atmosphere suddenly changed. A sweet, elegant fragrance filled the air. In the distance, Klifford could see the exit that led to the surface. And illuminating the path to the exit were rows of white blooms—Lieche orchids.

"You might say this was King Eus's obsession." The duke stopped in his tracks and gazed softly at the blooms. "For a time, King Eus was so eager to cultivate these flowers that he was said to have Lieche mania. One theory was that he had made plans to cover the entire castle at the time—Paradise in the Sky—in Lieche orchids. Though he never told anybody the reason why. But it was probably because"—the word hung in the air—"*because* he loved his sister so deeply. Thanks to Her Highness, I've realized that his reason was probably something as simple as that. King Eus did not like Lieche orchids, after all…"

Klifford's gaze fell upon Octavia's silvery tresses. The flowers that once adorned her hair now lay on the queen's blue cenotaph in tribute.

"Flowers for the late queen…," Leif Nightfellow murmured.

Enticed by the Lieche orchids, they walked the path to the exit. When they exited the cave, the royal carriage had already arrived. The soldiers were hard at work, assigning tasks.

The night breeze blew by. Octavia's eyes cracked open. "Klifford... Are you there?" She gripped Klifford's shirt with her right hand. She was only half awake.

"Yes, Princess. I am here."

Her aquamarine eyes looked up at him. Then she smiled with a relieved sigh...and closed her eyes again.

The junior ball was over. Now it was time to rest.

So it would be fair for him to make a wish— *May my Sovereign sleep peacefully.*

—Fin.

Afterword

And that was *Watashi wa Gotsugou Shugi na Kaiketsu Tantou no Oujo de Aru 3*—*WataGo* 3 for short. Thank you very much for reading it! Hi, I'm Mamecyoro.

Since the previous volume came out in 2018, it's been quite a long wait! We went from the Heisei era to Reiwa, too. And forgive me for going on a personal tangent, but I went through some drastic changes during that time period as well. But I've been writing a little bit every day while getting used to my new lifestyle, so I hope you'll bear with me.

Also, between the release of Volumes 2 and 3, on November 22, 2019, this series began its serialization as a comic. It's receiving rave reviews on the free webcomic sites ComicWalker, NicoNico Seiga, and pixiv Comic. It's published under the Flos Comic label. Kazusa Yoneda is doing great work on the manga—you really get to see Octavia and the other characters jump out on the page.

Expressing things is just so different in novels and manga. Whenever I read the manga, I always catch myself groaning about how the scenes I wrote one way in the novel changed so much in the manga! Though at times, I think *Gee, that's how I should've written that scene!* I'm honestly excited to read more of the manga as a fan.

Anyway, Volume 1 of the manga is going to be released the same month as Volume 3 of this light novel series. It's going to be released a bit ahead of this book, so I hope you'll give it a read, too. But for starters, I definitely recommend reading it in webcomic form!

Anyway, that's enough self-promo for now. Let's talk about Volume 3!

Volume 3 basically tied up the Junior Ball Arc. Even I was surprised by how long it turned out to be, but I was satisfied that I got to take the time to write the fight scene in the second half of the Junior Ball Arc. The back-and-forth with Rust and the search for Sil were the main focus.

When I first started picturing the story in my mind, I thought that the episodes pertaining to Sil would come much later, but since I added him to the junior ball, Alexis's daydreams and other things got pushed forward, too. That's right, even with the invasion, the junior ball storyline was supposed to end much earlier!

And as a result of that, Leif Nightfellow's grand entrance got moved to later, too. Just seeing the name on its own might make you go *Huh? Who's that again?* Well, he's the Uncle Dearest we got brief allusions to in Volumes 1 and 2. He's Uncle Dearest. Yes, I said that twice, even though it wasn't that important.

When he made his grand entrance through Octavia's POV, I thought *Hmm, he's like a belated hero! Boy, I sure did drag out introducing him, didn't I?!*

And Octavia never wound up finding her fake boyfriend at the junior ball, either!

Well, that *was* part of the plan.

As for the beautiful color illustration on the Volume 3 cover by Fuji, it just had to be Klifford in the white uniform. Fuji was so kind to put up with all the requests I made for the cover art and draw a perfect cover. The cover for Volume 3 truly is beautiful!

Lastly, the side story from Guy's POV was cut from the print version of this book. So if you're curious about what happened to Guy after the junior ball, check out "A Commoner Soldier Overanalyzes Everything—Here's His Probably Peaceful Day Off" on the web version! It makes a great supplemental story for the Junior Ball Arc…I hope.

Thank you to everyone who's read the series this far. I hope we get to meet again soon!

Mamecyoro

HAVE YOU BEEN TURNED ON TO LIGHT NOVELS YET?

86—EIGHTY-SIX, VOL. 1–11

In truth, there is no such thing as a bloodless war. Beyond the fortified walls protecting the eighty-five Republic Sectors lies the "nonexistent" Eighty-Sixth Sector. The young men and women of this forsaken land are branded the Eighty-Six and, stripped of their humanity, pilot "unmanned" weapons into battle...

Manga adaptation available now!

WOLF & PARCHMENT, VOL. 1–6

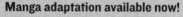

The young man Col dreams of one day joining the holy clergy and departs on a journey from the bathhouse, Spice and Wolf. Winfiel Kingdom's prince has invited him to help correct the sins of the Church. But as his travels begin, Col discovers in his luggage a young girl with a wolf's ears and tail named Myuri, who stowed away for the ride!

Manga adaptation available now!

SOLO LEVELING, VOL. 1–7

E-rank hunter Jinwoo Sung has no money, no talent, and no prospects to speak of—and apparently, no luck, either! When he enters a hidden double dungeon one fateful day, he's abandoned by his party and left to die at the hands of some of the most horrific monsters he's ever encountered.

Comic adaptation available now!

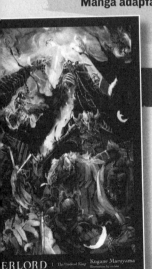